She studied the intruder more carefully, going beyond his startling good looks this time.

She noticed that despite the seeming rebelliousness of his hair, there was a stylish cut there.

Noticed that the watch on his left wrist was definitely out of her league.

Noticed that while the jeans and knit shirt he wore weren't blatantly expensive, the belt around his slim waist was.

Noticed that the athletic shoes he wore were past new, but a top brand.

Why?

Why would a good-looking guy who obviously wasn't down on his luck rent a room from an elderly couple in a tiny place like Summer Harbor? And be so darned nice to them to boot?

She could only think of one reason.

He was up to something.

Dear Reader,

It's fall and the kids are going back to school, which means more time for you to read. And you'll need all of it, because you won't want to miss a single one of this month's Silhouette Intimate Moments, starting with *In Broad Daylight*. This latest CAVANAUGH JUSTICE title from award winner Marie Ferrarella matches a badge-on-his-sleeve detective with a heart-on-her-sleeve teacher as they search for a missing student, along with something even rarer: love.

Don't Close Your Eyes as you read Sara Orwig's newest. This latest in her STALLION PASS: TEXAS KNIGHT miniseries features the kind of page-turning suspense no reader will want to resist as Colin Garrick returns to town with danger on his tail—and romance in his future. FAMILY SECRETS: THE NEXT GENERATION continues with *A Touch of the Beast*, by Linda Winstead Jones. Hawk Donovan and Sheryl Eldanis need to solve the mystery of the past or they'll have no shot at all at a future…together. Award-winning Justine Davis's hero has the heroine *In His Sights* in her newest REDSTONE, INCORPORATED title. Suspicion brings this couple together, but it's honesty and passion that will keep them there. A cursed pirate and a modern-day researcher are the unlikely—but perfect—lovers in Nina Bruhns's *Ghost of a Chance*, a book as wonderful as it is unexpected. Finally, welcome new author Lauren Giordano, whose debut novel, *For Her Protection*, tells an opposites-attract story with humor, suspense and plenty of irresistible emotion.

Enjoy them all—then come back next month for more of the best and most exciting romance reading around, only in Silhouette Intimate Moments.

Yours,

Leslie J. Wainger
Executive Editor

Please address questions and book requests to:
Silhouette Reader Service
U.S.: 3010 Walden Ave., P.O. Box 1325, Buffalo, NY 14269
Canadian: P.O. Box 609, Fort Erie, Ont. L2A 5X3

In His Sights
JUSTINE DAVIS

INTIMATE MOMENTS™
Published by Silhouette Books
America's Publisher of Contemporary Romance

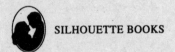 **SILHOUETTE BOOKS**

ISBN 0-373-27388-6

IN HIS SIGHTS

Visit Silhouette Books at www.eHarlequin.com

Printed in U.S.A.

Books by Justine Davis

Silhouette Intimate Moments

Hunter's Way #371
Loose Ends #391
Stevie's Chase #402
Suspicion's Gate #423
Cool Under Fire #444
Race Against Time #474
To Hold an Eagle #497
Target of Opportunity #506
One Last Chance #517
Wicked Secrets #555
Left at the Altar #596
Out of the Dark #638
The Morning Side of Dawn #674
*Lover Under Cover #698
*Leader of the Pack #728
*A Man To Trust #805
*Gage Butler's Reckoning #841
*Badge of Honor #871
*Clay Yeager's Redemption #926
The Return of Luke McGuire #1036
†Just Another Day in Paradise #1141
The Prince's Wedding #1190
†One of These Nights #1201
†In His Sights #1318

Silhouette Desire

Angel for Hire #680
Upon the Storm #712
Found Father #772
Private Reasons #833
Errant Angel #924
A Whole Lot of Love #1281
*Midnight Seduction #1557

Silhouette Bombshell

Proof #2

Silhouette Books

Silhouette Summer Sizzlers 1994
"The Raider"

Fortune's Children
The Wrangler's Bride

*Trinity Street West
†Redstone, Incorporated

JUSTINE DAVIS

lives on Puget Sound in Washington. She says that years ago, during her career in law enforcement, a young man she worked with encouraged her to try for a promotion to a position that was at the time occupied only by men. "I succeeded, became wrapped up in my new job, and that man moved away, never, I thought, to be heard from again. Ten years later he appeared out of the woods of Washington State, saying he'd never forgotten me and would I please marry him. With that history, how could I write anything but romance?"

Once upon a time, there was a genre of books that was sadly misunderstood by many people who didn't read them. Those who did read them loved them, cherished them, were changed by them. But still, these books got no respect on the outside, in fact were belittled, denigrated, held up as bad examples, while their readers and authors were sneered at and insulted by people who, although they never read the books, had somehow arrived at the idea that it was all right to slap others down for their choices. But those readers and authors kept on in the face of this horrible prejudice. Why? Because they found something in these books that they found nowhere else. Something precious, that spoke to them in a very deep and basic way.

Then one day, this beleaguered genre was given a gift. A fairy godmother if you will, a person with an incredible knowledge of these books and why they worked, and an even more incredible generosity of spirit. A one-person support system who gave so much to the writers of these stories, and was ever unselfish with her time and that amazing knowledge. And her endorsement counted for something; readers took her word and knew they would rarely be disappointed. She was a rock, a pillar on which the genre depended. Her loss has left a gaping hole that can never be filled, and will always be felt by those who love these books—and loved her.

For those reasons and so many more, the Redstone, Incorporated series is dedicated to

MELINDA HELFER

Lost to us August 24, 2000, but if heaven is what it should be she's in an endless library, with an eternity to revel in the books she loved. Happy reading, my friend....

Chapter 1

"**Y**ou'll just love him. He's the sweetest man. Absolutely charming."

Kate Crawford gaped at her grandmother. "You rented out a room? What room? To what man? Why?"

"My goodness, do you think you could string a few more questions together?"

Kate sat down, certain she wasn't understanding something. Her plans to make a grocery run for her grandparents were obviously going to have to wait.

"Gram," she said slowly, "what have you and Gramps done?"

"I told you," Dorothy Crawford said patiently, "we rented out our room."

"Your bedroom?"

"It's the only one that made sense, since it has the private bath and sitting area. We're thinking of using some of the income to add an outside stairway to the upper deck, then it will have its own private entrance as well."

"But—

"We're not using it, after all. The stairs are just too much for your grandfather's knees."

"I know that," Kate said.

And she did; she'd been the one to help them move into the one downstairs bedroom in the house. She hadn't liked the idea—the room was too small and the bathroom was way down the hall—but it had seemed the best temporary solution they could manage until they could afford to do a remodel. Or talk her grandfather into the knee replacement surgery he insisted he didn't want, a decision Kate suspected was also based on finances.

"If you needed money," Kate began, but stopped when her grandmother gave her the look she knew too well.

"We won't keep taking from you, Kate. You've done so much, too much, for us already."

"I could never do too much."

"And that's why your grandfather and I have to step in now and then, or you'd spend all your time and money on us, instead of having a life of your own."

"But—"

"No buts. Besides, it's done. We have a renter. We can't back out now."

And that brought Kate back to one of her initial questions. "Who is this person you've rented a room to? There's no one in town looking for a place that I know of."

In any place but Summer Harbor that might be a ridiculous statement, but here it was quite reasonable that if someone was looking for a place to live, everybody in town would know it. It was easy to keep track of such things when you only had a couple of thousand people to deal with.

"Oh, he's not from here."

That alone was enough for Kate, and her voice was rather sharp when she demanded, "Where is he from, and what's he doing here?"

"I believe he's a photographer," her grandmother said. "And I can do without that tone, young lady."

Chastened, Kate reached out and put a hand over Dorothy's. "I'm sorry, Gram. You know I just worry."

"You worry too much," Dorothy said, but the stern tone had been replaced by a lovingly gentle one. "This is Summer Harbor, you know. Bad things don't happen here."

Tell that to Joshua Redstone, Kate thought.

The thievery at Redstone Northwest had already come to the attention of the multibillionaire entrepreneur who owned the business, and while she doubted there was another boss of his stature who would care, she knew Josh Redstone was different. Very different. It was one of the many reasons she loved her job there.

"Ah, good," her grandmother said at the sound of a tap on the door, "here he is now, so you'll get to meet him. Then you'll see there's no problem."

Kate turned, expecting the man to walk right in. But he politely waited for her grandmother to call out to him.

"Come on in, Rand."

Since Dorothy Crawford was hardly one to call a man by his last name unless it was preceded by a Mister, Kate had to assume Rand was his first name. She turned to look at the door as it swung open.

She wasn't sure what she'd been expecting, but this wasn't it. The man who came in was, in a word, beautiful. Young, but beautiful. Six feet or better, with hair a shade of platinum blond she'd only seen on children until now. It was thick and a bit unruly, falling forward over his forehead in the same way a child's silky hair did.

But while young, he was anything but a child. He moved with a very male kind of grace that told her he was probably an athlete of some kind, or at least in good shape.

Very good shape, she amended wryly as she got a better look.

"No point in you knocking if you're going to be living here," her grandmother was saying. "Just come on in."

The man glanced at Kate before he answered her grandmother, and Kate felt an odd little jolt at the sight of vivid, cobalt-blue eyes.

Oh, now that really wasn't fair. Not fair at all.

Then he smiled, not at her but at her grandmother, and Kate instantly went on guard.

"I stopped at the market for some things," he said, "so I picked up the sugar you said you'd forgotten."

"Well, wasn't that sweet of you?" Dorothy cooed.

Her grandmother actually cooed, Kate thought, barely managing to resist shaking her head in shock. That sort of reaction was usually limited to babies and puppies. Certainly not grown men. And for all his boyish looks, there was no mistaking this Rand was just that. He looked to only be in his twenties, but he was still all man.

"Gram," she began, unable to stop the urge to caution that rose in her.

"Ah. You must be Kate," the man said. "I should have guessed."

Instantly provoked, and not quite sure why, Kate went on the offensive. "And why is that, Mr….?"

"Singleton," he supplied politely. "Rand Singleton, Miss Crawford."

He made her feel like a schoolteacher, with that very

proper "miss." An old schoolteacher. But if he thought that would distract her, he was mistaken.

"Why would you assume I'm Kate?" she persisted.

"Because," he said with a smile at her grandmother, "beauty seems to run in the family."

Oh, good grief, Kate thought. *He can't think anybody's buying this!*

Then she caught a glimpse of her grandmother's face and, astonishingly, the spots of color rising in her cheeks. Her jaw dropped. Her grandmother, it seemed, was buying it by the bagful.

Her eyes narrowed as she turned them on the newcomer. He met her gaze steadily, with one brow lifted as if he knew exactly what she was thinking.

I don't care if you do, she muttered inwardly.

"If you doubt that," he said softly, clearly aimed at her, "you need a new mirror."

"And you need a new line," she said as her grandmother smiled with obvious pleasure.

She had a mirror, and she knew perfectly well what she looked like. Average. Nice eyes, although of late they were tired and bloodshot more often than not. Hair was okay, kind of a nondescript dark brown, but healthy and shiny even if simply clipping back the shoulder-length strands was her only effort at a hairstyle.

No, nothing striking or eye-catching about her, not these days. There had been a time, in the big corporate world and with the help of polished makeup, chic haircuts and stylish clothes, that she had drawn that kind of attention, but no longer. She didn't look bad for a woman of forty-one, but she was still average.

And still old enough to be this guy's…aunt.

She nearly laughed aloud at her own absurdity. The

man must have seen the change in her expression, for his own changed to one of puzzlement.

No, I haven't changed my mind about you, she said to herself in answer to his look. *I'm just realizing I'm as touchy as any woman of a certain age confronted with an attractive man too young for her. Especially when he seems to be flirting.*

Which was, of course, her imagination. Whatever he was doing, it likely had very little to do with her. And everything to do with charming her grandmother, who was chatting away as if this man had grown up next door.

She studied the intruder more carefully, going beyond his startling good looks this time. She noticed that despite the seeming rebelliousness of his hair, there was a stylish cut there. Noticed that the watch on his left wrist was, while not a Rolex, definitely out of her league. Noticed that while the jeans and knit shirt he wore weren't blatantly expensive, the belt around his slim waist was. Noticed that the athletic shoes he wore were past new, but a top brand.

Why?

Why would a good-looking, twenty-something guy, who obviously wasn't down on his luck, rent a room from an elderly couple in a tiny place like Summer Harbor? And be so darned nice to them to boot?

She could only think of one reason. He was up to something. And the most likely thing was trying to con her loving, generous grandparents. It was in the news almost every day—some poor, sweet grandmother or grandfather who had been taken in by a smooth operator. And that was something she would never, ever allow to happen. To her, people who scammed the elderly were beyond redemption. Anyone who would try to steal from the couple who had raised her, who had changed their entire life's plan for her, was going to have to deal with her. And she would not be kind.

"What are you doing in Summer Harbor?" Kate asked during the first pause in her grandmother's animated conversation, not caring if her bluntness offended him.

"Working," he said, the charming smile still in place, but his reaction clear in the one-word answer. Oddly, that reassured her. If he'd acted as if her nearly rude query were normal, she'd have been even more convinced he was up to no good.

"You're a photographer?" She reined in her tone a little, aware her grandmother was not looking pleased with her.

"This is a beautiful part of the world, worth photographing, don't you think?"

Well, there's an answer that avoids answering, she thought. "Freelance, I suppose," she muttered, knowing the answer. If he said he worked for some established magazine or publisher, it would be too easy to check. Her suspicions deepened.

"I do some freelance work, yes," he said, eyeing her steadily, almost as if he had suspicions of his own. "I like to make my own choices of what to photograph."

"And I'll bet you've been all over the world," Dorothy said. Almost gushed, Kate admitted ruefully.

"I've logged some miles," he agreed.

"You and Kate should talk. She used to travel a great deal. She was a big executive with an investment company back east."

"I don't think Denver qualifies as 'back east,' Gram," Kate said.

"It's east of here," the man said, turning a smile on Dorothy that would have melted the heart of any woman.

Except one who was afraid for the people she loved most in the world.

"Exactly," Dorothy said with obvious delight. "Come have a cup of coffee, now that there's sugar to put in it."

Oh, good grief, Kate thought again as the man followed her grandmother into the kitchen. She nearly said it aloud, then realized that if he was what she suspected, she'd best not antagonize him right off the bat. Better to let him think he was succeeding, and catch him in the act. She'd just have to watch him carefully.

That won't be too painful, she thought, then immediately castigated herself for being beyond stupid. Besides, even though it might not be painful, it was going to be a pain. She didn't have *time* for this. She already had those thefts at work to deal with. Plus her best mechanic, who'd lost his wife last year, was in a state of total distraction over his rebellious son. And then her grandparents needed a more reliable car to replace their old station wagon, and neither they nor she could afford it just now....

Which was why they'd decided to rent out a room, she realized suddenly. And felt guilty; they'd done so much for her. They'd taken her in and raised her at a time when they'd been looking forward to retiring, and then they'd taken her back again when her world had fallen apart. She owed them everything, and had paid them back so little. They'd argue with her, of course, and mean it. They'd done it out of love, but that didn't lessen her worry that she wasn't taking good enough care of them.

"I gather you didn't know about this?"

The quiet voice behind her startled her. She spun around to see the new boarder watching her as he sipped from one of her grandmother's favorite coffee mugs.

She tried to rein in her antagonism, but it was fueled by worry and she wasn't very successful. "About this plan to rent a room in their own home? No, I didn't."

"And you don't like it."

She noticed it wasn't a question, but supposed her demeanor had made that obvious to all but the thickest bricks. He clearly wasn't one of those. But she supposed you didn't make a good con artist if you couldn't sense what your victims were feeling.

"No," she said, reverting to bluntness once more.

"Fortunate for me, then, that it's not your decision."

He turned then and walked back into the kitchen, leaving Kate gaping after him.

After a moment she closed her mouth.

You'd think a con man would be a little more careful about offending, she thought. Which led to the obvious thought that perhaps, just perhaps, he wasn't one.

Or, she amended, he was just a very good one, and knew better than to appear *too* ingratiating.

"Whatever you're up to, you're not going to get away with it," she muttered as she picked up her keys. "I'll see to that."

Somehow, she added silently. *Along with everything else I have to do, I'll see to it.*

Chapter 2

Kate Crawford was nervous, Rand Singleton thought.

She was also beautiful. Not in the way of the photos he'd seen in her personnel file, where she was glamorous, gorgeous and looked very high-power, but in a much more natural way. More real. More reachable. More.

Touchable, he thought, then shook his head at his own folly. It didn't matter what she looked like. Didn't matter that her hair was sleek and shiny and the color of rich, dark coffee. Or that her eyes were unexpectedly topaz and quite striking. Or that she was tall and graceful with just the right amount of curves. What mattered was the fact that she clearly didn't like the idea of him being here at all.

He mentally filed the knowledge away. This assignment was just beginning, so he wasn't sure where—or if—she fit in yet. What he was sure of was that she was in the perfect position at Redstone Northwest to be involved, or even be the mastermind behind the thefts. Especially since they had begun shortly after she'd started working there.

That's why he'd been so pleased with his luck. He'd planned to just stay in a local motel, figuring it would work for his cover as a photographer. Little had he known that the town of Summer Harbor didn't have a motel. Not this time of year, anyway; the small guest operations that were open during the tourist-filled summer months were closed now, many of the owners fleeing south ahead of the approaching winter.

"Teach you to assume," he told himself as he finished unpacking in the comfortably sized upstairs room, furnished with older but quality pieces that made him feel as if he was staying back at his own grandparents' suburban home outside San Diego.

He smothered the pang he always felt when he thought of the two people who had loved him so. He still missed them, and the only thing that eased the pain was the knowledge that they had died as they had lived for so many years; together. Dorothy and Walt Crawford reminded him of them, and he'd felt immediately comfortable with the couple. And, as usually happened, they seemed to take to him right off. Sometimes this innocent baby face of his was an advantage.

He'd chosen the armoire as a storage place for his photographic gear. He handled the equipment with the familiarity of long usage. He'd once considered becoming a photographer in fact, but the lure of working for Redstone, Inc. had been too much, and once he'd landed on the crack Redstone security team, he knew he'd found his true calling.

His mother hadn't been happy about it, knowing he would occasionally be sent on risky assignments, but she'd finally backed off, saying that if he was going to have such an insane career, it might as well be for Joshua Redstone, who was known for looking out for his people.

Josh also made sure Rand had a chance to do some photography work now and then, some of which had been used around the world in Redstone literature and advertising, and Rand felt as if he had the very best of two worlds.

When he'd finished with the photo gear, he turned to the rest of the things he'd packed. He tossed the jeans in a dresser drawer along with a couple of pullover sweaters and several shirts. He had a feeling he would be glad he'd taken Josh's advice and put in some heavy socks. The days were still warm, but the brisk scent of winter was already in the evening air up here in the Northwest, although the actual turn of the season was still a couple of weeks away.

The sound of singing from downstairs brought him back to his original thought about his luck. What else would you call it when you stumbled into the perfect setup—a room for rent by the family of the head of the very Redstone department he'd been sent to investigate?

When the man at the small grocery had mentioned that the Crawfords were looking for a tenant, it had seemed so lucky that he'd been suspicious at first, until he realized that in a town with a year-round population of less than two thousand, it was likely everybody really did know everybody else's business.

There didn't seem to be much buzz about anything going on at Redstone, though. He'd felt his way very carefully, saying only that he'd seen the place while out exploring the countryside. The only reaction he'd gotten was one of open, cheerful enthusiasm for the presence of Redstone. It had apparently done wonders for the tax base of the tiny town, thanks to some bargaining Joshua Redstone had done with the county, making sure a large portion of the taxes they would pay would go directly to Summer Harbor.

But now someone was stealing from the benefactor. And although to some the crimes might seem petty when weighed against the vastness of the Redstone empire, Josh was not one to let things like this slide or consider them beneath his attention. Especially when what was being stolen was one of Redstone inventor Ian Gamble's latest inventions. The new self-regulating, automatic insulin pump functioned like a normal pancreas because it could sense when the body needed insulin and automatically administer it. It could not only save thousands of lives, but make thousands more easier.

Of course, that made it even more valuable to the thieves.

Rand finished unpacking the last of his clothes and stood for a moment, contemplating whether he was going to need the heavy parka he'd just hung up in the closet. He decided against it for now, figuring he'd get the feel of the temperature first. He'd just been in Canada last week, so perhaps he was still acclimated somewhat to the cooler clime.

Sure he'd left his small .38 revolver securely locked in the case for now, he was done. He dug his cell phone out of the side pocket of the duffle that had held everything he'd brought, including his laptop. He hit the button that had been programmed to dial Redstone Security at their California headquarters.

"Draven."

"It's Rand," he said to his boss, head of Redstone security. "I'm in place."

"Good."

Man of very few words, his boss. "You'll never guess where."

"No, I won't."

Rand sighed; John Draven seemed edgier than usual today, which was saying something.

"Crawford's grandparent's."

There was a pause, and Rand thought with some satisfaction that for once he'd surprised the unflappable Draven.

"They were renting out a room," he added, feeling he should.

"Convenient," was all Draven said.

"Yeah, I wondered about that, especially finding out about it like I did. But the town's so small, everybody knows everything."

"Different."

"Very," Rand agreed.

"Your cover going to work?"

Rand had been offered a cover inside the Redstone facility here, but had decided it might work better if he was on the outside. Besides, there was a new security guy on board at this plant, Brian Fisher, a kid Josh himself had hired. He had been trying to investigate the thefts, and Josh didn't want the twenty-two-year-old's confidence crushed. So Rand had taken out the camera gear that had sat unused for too long and headed for the rural Northwest undercover.

"I think so," he said. "Josh is right, it's beautiful up here. It's the kind of place that draws photographers like flies."

"So does dead meat," Draven said dryly.

"Yeah, yeah," Rand retorted, long used to the man's off center sense of humor. "I'd better get started if I'm going to find out what's making those insulin pumps magically disappear between the time the trucks are loaded and delivery is made, with no sign of break-ins."

"I don't believe in magic."

"No, I don't suppose you do."

Rand knew what John Draven did believe in. He'd asked him once. The answer had been Josh Redstone, the randomness of life and the stopping power of a .45.

"Report when you have something to say," Draven said.

"As usual," Rand said, smothering a wry grin. Draven was nothing if not a master of brevity.

He understood, though. It had been a rough couple of years for Redstone when it came to employees. And that was unusual enough that Josh was a little touchy on the subject. He chose his people carefully, then gave them free rein to do what they did best, and it very rarely backfired on him.

But this bad stretch had begun with Bill Talbert, the employee Draven had caught feathering his own nest at the expense of guests at one of the Redstone resorts. Then Phil Cooper, found only in death to have been slime to his wife and son if not to Redstone itself. And just a few months ago, corporate secrets from Ian Gamble's research being sold to a competitor by someone inside. Considering the size of Redstone, it wasn't all that much, but Josh tended to take such betrayals personally.

And he wasn't the only one—everybody at Redstone circled the wagons when someone tried to damage the place they all loved so much. Josh was the kind of man who inspired a loyalty that couldn't be bought, and every last one of the security team was dedicated to keeping things just the way he liked them: honest, clean and profitable.

Josh had made liars of many who insisted the three couldn't exist together in the business world. Rand wasn't about to let that change, not even out here in one of the smaller Redstone outposts. He'd find out who the thief was, and they'd come face-to-face with the other Redstone inexorable—justice.

As she did almost every morning she went to work, Kate paused after she turned off the road and into the driveway of Redstone Northwest. It seemed a small miracle, this place. Joshua Redstone had insisted a manufacturing plant could be built without destroying the countryside, and he'd proved it here.

Redstone Northwest looked more like an exclusive hunting lodge than a factory. Each building was clad in siding milled from the trees they'd had to clear. The entrance drive curved through big trees that had been intentionally left standing to mask the actual size of the building. It made bringing bigger supply trucks in and out a challenge, but when that point had been brought up to Josh he had merely nodded and said if the driver couldn't do it, he shouldn't be driving for Redstone, and if he wouldn't do it, he didn't understand Redstone.

When she'd been interviewed for this job by the great Josh Redstone himself—in a process that had seemed more like a casual conversation than a job interview—he'd concluded their meeting by asking if she had any questions. The one that was obvious to her slipped out before she could stop it.

"Why here?" she had asked. "Why did you build a Redstone facility here, in tiny Summer Harbor?" She loved the little town she'd recently moved back to, but still wondered why a company the size of Redstone had located here.

"You don't like it being here?" the lanky, gray-eyed man had asked, not in a challenging tone but in the way of someone genuinely interested.

"No, no," she'd said quickly. "I'm happy you decided to build here. It's been great, done wonders for the town. I'm just curious. We're sort of at the crossroads of nowhere and can't get there from here."

Josh had laughed, and Kate had found herself smiling at the sound of it. She'd done a little research before she'd applied for the job, and had read that the man didn't laugh often anymore. Rumor had it that the death of his wife a few years ago had taken the laughter right out of him. That she'd managed to make him do it pleased her much more than she would have thought, given she'd only just met the man.

"Perhaps for just that reason," he said.

"Whatever your reason, I'm glad," she told him. "And I would love to be part of it."

He had gestured at her résumé, on the table in front of him. In what she had since come to learn was typical Josh Redstone fashion, he had chosen to conduct interviews outside. She had arrived for this interview to find one of the richest men in the world seated at an ordinary card table under a large madrone tree in front of the building that was still being finished.

"You're a bit overqualified," he'd said.

She hadn't argued that, she knew it was true and wouldn't insult his intelligence by denying it.

"But I'm a *lot* overqualified for any other job in town," she had said. "And I'm staying here, no matter what, so I'd like the most challenging job I can get."

Josh Redstone had studied her for a long, silent moment. So long that she'd wondered if she should have been so blunt. Finally he'd stood up and held out a hand to her.

"Welcome to Redstone, Ms. Crawford."

And so now here she was, she thought as she finally continued on to the parking area on the far side of the build-

ing, distribution manager for Redstone Northwest. And
while it wasn't the high-power, moving-millions-of-
dollars-a-day job she'd held in Denver, it was enough to
keep her mind sharp. Even more important, it let her stay
in Summer Harbor, to take care of her grandparents. And
right now that was the most important thing in the world
to her.

She pulled into her usual parking spot, the one she'd
picked at the far end of the lot, although she could have had
one with her name on it closer to the doors. She wanted
this one to add a bit more exercise to her crowded days.
The extra walking, coupled with lunch breaks frequently
spent in the small basement gym Redstone had built, kept
her in shape and the sneaky extra pounds off.

"Too much stuff," she muttered to herself, not for the
first time as she gathered up her purse and heavy satchel.
The canvas bag that held both ends of her record keeping
spectrum—her traditional clipboard and her more modern
PDA—was a far cry from the elegant leather briefcase she
had once carried. But it was far more practical—and less
conspicuous—here in the casual Northwest.

She headed for her office, remembering how joyous her
first months here had been. In fact, her work here had been
immensely satisfying, and the longer she worked for Redstone the more she liked it. And the idea of someone stealing from the company made her very angry.

Furthermore, the idea that what they were stealing was
being taken from people who desperately needed the help
of Redstone's newest invention turned that anger to fury.
It was a fury tempered only by apprehension; she had some
suspicions about who might be involved in this string of
thefts—if two could be called a string—and she didn't at
all like the possibility that she'd come up with.

As she turned down the hall and headed for her office, nodding and greeting the staff she encountered, she renewed her determination to put a stop to this. Josh had opened this facility here because he loved the area and wanted to help the local economy, and she didn't want him to ever regret it. She felt as if the reputation of Summer Harbor was at stake. She would not let what had so far been a small problem become a large one for Redstone.

To her surprise, when she got to her office the usually locked door was already open. She took another step forward. Not only that, but there was someone inside and that someone was sitting at her computer.

The computer where the schedules for the shipments of the insulin pumps were stored.

Chapter 3

Kate stepped into her office quietly. There was no mistaking who the unexpected occupant was; the maroon streaks in her brown hair didn't leave much room for mistakes.

Kate watched for a moment before speaking. There was a spreadsheet on the computer screen, but she couldn't see from here which one it was.

"Mel?"

"Oh!" Melissa Morris spun around, clearly startled. "Ms. Crawford, I didn't hear you."

"Looking for something?" Kate asked, not taking her eyes off the girl while she set down her purse and canvas bag. It wasn't unusual for the girl to be there, but Kate was touchy these days.

"Yes. Those old shipping numbers. So I can finish that practice analysis you wanted." She looked embarrassed. "I lost my copy."

Kate relaxed. Inwardly, although she knew her critical data password was protected, she was grateful there was such an innocent explanation for Mel's presence and her actions. Outwardly, she frowned. "Don't you have a term paper to finish?"

The sixteen-year-old, who had adopted the nickname of Mel for the hated Melissa years ago, nodded. "But I keep getting them confused. If I sit down to work on the paper, I think of the analysis report. If I sit down to work on the report, all I can think about is the term paper."

Kate, who could remember being in a very similar position in school more than once, smiled. "The brain sometimes sabotages you, doesn't it? No matter how hard you try to focus on one thing, other things keep sneaking in."

Mel gave her a look that trumpeted her relief that Kate understood. "Yes, exactly."

"So, what are you going to do?"

Mel hesitated. "Aren't you supposed to tell me that?"

Kate smiled. "The mentor program is supposed to give you the chance to learn. Sometimes the best way to do that is fight through to the answers yourself. And learn how to do that." She shrugged. "I'm just here to nudge if you head down a wrong path."

"Oh." The girl looked disconcerted for a moment, then thoughtful. "Well, while I was trying to do my term paper, I had some ideas about a different way to do the distribution analysis I thought were good. So I came here to get that done, while the ideas were fresh in my mind."

"All right," Kate said. "But you need to balance that. We don't want the work experience counselor revoking your privilege to spend mornings here. Tonight you work only on your paper."

The girl perked up. "Okay. I think maybe I can finish

the rough numbers today, and that will be enough to get it out of my head so I can concentrate on my paper."

"If you can't get around the roadblock, sometimes you just have to tear it down," Kate said.

Mel's nose wrinkled. "Is that another one of your grandfather's old sayings?"

Kate grinned. "Yep. He prefers to think of them as axioms of wisdom."

"Is that a weapon of some kind, an axiom?"

"It can be," Kate said. "Look it up when you're done with your paper," Kate added.

"Yeah," the girl said, then sighed somewhat morosely. "So, where can I find those shipping figures?"

"They're in the distribution spreadsheet. It hasn't been closed out for the quarter yet, so it's in the open files."

"Okay. I'll move out to the other computer."

"I've got some manifests to work on, so if you want to use mine, you can have it for about a half hour."

"Great! It's hard to concentrate out there," she said, gesturing toward the outer office where Kate's assistant had his desk, and held vendors, salespeople and job seekers at bay until their appointment times.

A few minutes later Mel's maroon-streaked head was bent over the keyboard as she brought up the spreadsheet she needed. When the student started working here, she hadn't been familiar with the software program Redwood used, but she knew computers and had quickly figured it out. The girl was bright enough, quite, in fact, but she was also chafing against the restraints of living in a small town that didn't even have a movie theater. Kate had recognized the signs, which was why she'd offered herself as the girl's mentor when she'd signed up for the program at her school.

Why Mel had accepted, she wasn't quite sure. There had

been people in other parts of the county who had volunteered for the mentoring program, places where there was much more of what Mel called "civilization." But she'd chosen Kate, right here in Summer Harbor, the very place she wanted so desperately to escape.

And that, Kate thought, was the first thing that had made her suspicious. That and the occasional flash of anger she saw in the girl, anger at being stuck here in the place she derided with a very descriptive and obscene term. Kate had had to tell her she could curse up a storm anywhere else she could get away with it, but not inside Redstone. And then realized she was going to have to live up to her own rules and rein in the occasional "damn" that escaped her.

But when the thefts had started, she'd wondered. Wondered if there was another reason Mel had chosen her as the person she wanted as her mentor. If perhaps it wasn't her, or her work that had attracted the girl at all, but Redstone, and getting on the inside. Kate didn't like thinking that way, but she couldn't help the questions that popped into her mind when the girl complained about tiny Summer Harbor.

Now that would be just peachy, she thought sourly, *if she'd actually invited the thief into the nest, as it were.*

She turned to look at the girl again. "Mel?" The teenager looked up. "Why did you pick me?"

"What do you mean?"

"You could have picked someone in L.A., Chicago or even Seattle. The kind of place you want to go. But you chose me, here."

Mel nodded.

"Why?"

"Because you got out. Those others were always there, so they didn't have anywhere to get out of. But you did, and you got out, even if you came back. That's what I wanted to learn."

It made a certain kind of sense, Kate thought. Teenage sense, but sense.

Of course, that didn't mean she wasn't involved in the thefts. It could just mean that part came later.

Kate began to sort the cargo manifests. As she organized them, part of her mind was still, as it had been since the start of this trouble, occupied with trying to solve the riddle of the thefts.

"Kate? Oh, she's a good one," the grocer said with a smile. "Not many who'd leave a big career like she had and come home to take care of her grandparents when they started having health problems."

"Is that why she did it?" Rand had dropped by to thank the man for pointing him toward the Crawford's room for rent, and had grabbed the chance to pump him a bit, since he seemed more than willing to talk.

"Well, she'll tell you she got homesick, didn't like the big-city life."

"Some don't," Rand said neutrally, even as he was thinking that going from Denver to this small town would be more than a major adjustment.

"I know I couldn't take it," the man behind the counter agreed, his tone a bit fervent. "Lived over in Seattle for a while, and even that about made me crazy."

"But you don't think that's Kate's real reason?" Rand gently nudged the conversation back in the direction he needed.

"Well, it may be true she didn't like the city, but the real reason is she loves her grandparents and knows they need her now."

Well, that's noble, I guess, Rand thought. *Too noble to be believed?*

He didn't know.

"So, she wasn't running away from any trouble or anything?"

The grocer's expression suddenly changed. His eyes narrowed, all trace of the warm, small-town welcome vanished now. "Kate's not the kind to run from trouble, if she were the kind to get into trouble in the first place."

Rand knew immediately he'd made a mistake. Hastily, he backpedaled. "It just seemed she was a bit edgy, when I met her. I didn't want to make it worse by saying something out of ignorance."

"Oh. Well. Then."

The man stopped short of an actual apology, but his demeanor quickly shifted back to the genial storekeeper.

Hmm, Rand thought as he purchased a soda and departed.

His next stop was the only other establishment of any size in town, a carries-everything hardware store. He got much the same reaction there; open friendliness, liking for Kate Crawford and an instant withdrawal behind a screen of seeming protectiveness at the slightest suggestion she was anything less than a beloved local girl who made good and then came home.

It was the same everywhere, although admittedly the options were few; the small drugstore, the smaller post office, the yet smaller soup and sandwich café. He even braced himself and stepped into a shop labeled Curl and Cut, which smelled of some hair chemical that made his eyes water. He covered his presence by saying he would be staying in Summer Harbor for a while and wanted to know if they cut men's hair.

"For you, honey, you bet," the matronly blond woman

wearing a black plastic apron said with a wink so broad he couldn't keep from grinning back at her. "I'd love to get my hands into that hair. I'm Esther."

"Hi, Esther. I'm Rand. I'm renting a room at the Crawford's."

The woman's smile became even broader. "Oh, that's good. I know they were looking to do that. They're good people, they'll take care of you."

He hesitated, aware of several women in the place, in various stages of what looked like strange and exotic treatments, then plunged ahead. "I like them. I don't think their granddaughter likes me, though."

"Kate? Now that's odd, she likes most people. She's the sweetest girl. Glad she's back here where she belongs, especially after what she's been through. Whatever made you think she didn't like you?"

He decided on the concerned approach this time. "She's not in any trouble, is she? Is that why she's a bit edgy?"

"Kate, in trouble? Not likely," the woman replied, complete certainty in her tone. "If she's edgy, it's because she's worried. Her grandparents have had some money trouble, and they're not getting any younger, so their health is on her mind."

"Well," Rand amended, "maybe it wasn't just me, but the whole idea of me renting a room from her grandparents."

"Well, that could be. She's very protective of them. But I'd think she'd be glad to see a handsome, eligible young man around." The woman waggled an eyebrow at him. "You are eligible, aren't you?"

"For several things," Rand said.

She laughed. "Oh, Kate'll like you, all right. She's got a weakness for wit."

He smiled and thanked the woman, then turned to escape from the chemical smell and the interested gazes of the other women. He wondered if he'd be a topic at several dinner tables in Summer Harbor tonight. This small-town stuff was going to take some getting used to. He'd dealt with it in villages around the world, but somehow he'd never come up against it here at home.

Is anyone that *perfect?* he wondered as he got back in the small SUV he'd rented for the duration. *Did everybody in this town think Kate Crawford walked on water?*

It wasn't until he got to the single gas station to fill up that he got his answer to that.

"Oh, you mean Miss-too-good-for-the-likes-of-us?" The man in the grease-stained overalls, with the patch reading Scott, wiped his hands across his chest, depositing even more grease.

Rand's radar flipped into search mode. The man had wandered out from the garage when he'd pulled up to the pumps, as if he'd been waiting for someone to come in. After listening to him gripe about the weather and the people who complained about the price of gas, Rand had steered the man to the topic he wanted. And had gotten the first negative comment in town about Kate Crawford.

"Came back from the east a little snooty, did she?" he asked casually, keeping his eyes on the pump nozzle but also watching Scott out of the corner of his eye.

The man snickered. "It's those Redstone people, they think they own the world."

Whoa, Rand thought. *Where'd that come from?*

Scott sniffed audibly. "What's that? Smells like ammonia or something."

"It's probably me," Rand said, ruefully amazed it was still discernable over the gasoline fumes. "I stuck my nose in the Curl and Cut for directions."

Scott picked at a greasy fingernail as he laughed. "That'll teach you. You can smell that Esther coming for miles. Good thing, since she insists on butting into everybody else's business. Old hen."

A small Japanese sedan went by, stereo booming out bass so loud it shook the metal price sign out at the curb.

"Damn kids," Scott snarled. "Think everybody wants to listen to their crap."

"It was loud," Rand agreed mildly.

"Call that music, too. Stupid idiots. They're as bad as those high-falutin' classical snobs, with all that music by dead guys."

Ah, Rand thought. *I get it now. It wasn't Kate or Redstone in particular, this guy just hates the world. Guess there's one in every town, even one this small.*

He paid for his gas and pulled out of the station. Tank now full, he decided to explore a little, get the lay of the land, particularly around Redstone. As he drove, he thought about something Esther of the Curl and Cut—or was it Cut and Curl?—had said.

Glad she's back here where she belongs...

That seemed to be the consensus around here. Kate Crawford may have left Summer Harbor, but they'd clearly never forgotten her. And when she'd returned they had welcomed her with open arms.

The rest of what Esther had said came back to him then.

...especially after what she's been through.

He knew, from the file he'd read at Redstone headquarters before he'd come here, that Kate had been married once, and had lost a child to illness. Maybe that, he thought now, was the reason for that circle the wagons feeling he was getting. But that had been years ago. And she'd left

Summer Harbor long before that, and only come back in the wake of that tragic loss.

Or maybe it was simply the dynamic of a small town.

Rand shook his head in wonder. He'd been around the world, been in cities, villages and places even smaller than Summer Harbor, where the nearest civilization was hundreds of miles away, but he'd never spent a lot of time in small-town America. And while he couldn't deny the sheer beauty of this part of the world, this kind of tightly knit community already had him completely bemused.

He thought about what he'd learned about Kate Crawford this morning. That for the most part, Summer Harbor loved her. And that she had been, at most, a bit edgy of late. Hardly enough to convict someone for theft.

But added to the fact that she had motive—apparent financial problems—and opportunity, it was enough to keep her way up on the suspect list.

And if he didn't care for the idea, it was only because he already liked her grandparents. He didn't like thinking about what it would do to them to find out their granddaughter was a thief.

He checked once more on the gun lockbox under the seat. His two-inch .38 was inside to avoid discovery, and he hoped fervently he wouldn't have to use it.

Chapter 4

"No, not that one, silly boy! Don't you know a weed when you see it?"

"Apparently not," Rand said with a grin as he released the threatened plant.

He'd been working in the backyard with Dorothy ever since he'd returned from his exploration. He'd figured it would be a good way to keep an eye on Kate since she spent so much time here, but he was soon enjoying himself.

"My mom used to say a weed was just a plant growing where you didn't want it to," he said.

Dorothy laughed. "Well, she's right. Do you see her often, Rand?"

"Not often enough," he said. "But it's not all my fault. She and my dad retired and they're off globe-trotting more than they're home these days."

"Oh, how nice," Dorothy said. She left it at that, but

Rand had the feeling "for them" had followed in her mind. She was just too polite to say it aloud.

"This one goes?" He gestured at the next questionable plant he saw. At her nod he began to dig out the offender as he continued the conversation. "You don't like to travel?"

"Oh, we go to the coast now and then, and we used to go down to California in the winter, and up to Canada in the spring, but we love home the best so we stay here most of the time now."

He wondered if they had had to curtail their travels for health reasons or financial reasons. He'd brought in the mail for them—their mail box was out at the end of a very long driveway—when he'd returned from his first recon of the area. He had noticed several windowed envelopes that made Dorothy frown when she saw them. But she'd merely put them away with a sigh in a desk cubby that held several more of what appeared to be the same kind of envelopes.

Definitely motive, he thought, yanking out a dandelion rather fiercely at the thought that Kate might have had to resort to stealing to help these sweet people.

Well, Dorothy was sweet, anyway; Walter Crawford was a bit of a curmudgeon. Rand got the sense the silver-haired man with the bushy moustache used the gruffness to hide a too-soft heart, but he was honest enough to realize he might be projecting his memory of his own grandfather onto this man who somewhat resembled Robert Singleton.

"You really don't have to help me with this chore," Dorothy said.

Rand tossed the excavated weed into the trash bag they were dragging around with them. "I don't mind. Unless you'd rather do it all yourself. I can understand that. My mom used to feel like that sometimes. She said the only thing that kept her sane was working in her garden."

"And what was threatening to drive her insane?" Dorothy asked, with a sly grin that told Rand she was already guessing the answer.

"Yeah, yeah," he said, but he grinned back at her.

He had likely had the most normal family life of any of the Redstone security team, and his choice of careers had made his mother crazy. His father, at least, had understood, but then, he'd been a cop for nearly two decades before Rand's mother had prevailed upon him to retire—something he hadn't been that reluctant to do, saying all the good feelings had been driven out of the job anyway by the holes in the system and too many losing battles.

But Rand couldn't deny what Dorothy had said was true, most of the time it had been he himself who had driven his mother to the brink. If it hadn't been for Josh, who had, to Rand's shock, invited his entire family in to tour Redstone headquarters and then have lunch with him while he convinced them that he would look out for their only son, his mother would have made his life unbearable with her worrying.

But Josh had convinced them, and while Rand didn't tell his mother everything, he'd never been seriously hurt on an assignment for Redstone. Of course, his mother's opinion of what constituted seriously hurt might differ slightly from his, he admitted silently.

"Are you an only child?" Dorothy asked as they moved on to a shady flower bed full of what she told him were hostas and fuchsias.

"No, I've got a little sister. My mom said after my terrible twos she was sure there was never going to be another one. Took her nearly ten years to change her mind and have Lisa."

"Are you and your sister close?"

"Pretty much," he said. "I tried to always look out for her as a kid, although it was tough when I was sixteen having a six-year-old trailing after me."

"I can imagine," Dorothy said with a laugh. "Your friends must have loved to tease you."

"That they did," he agreed, thinking for the first time in years of the one friend who had gone way too far with his teasing.

"Oh, that was an unpleasant thought," Dorothy said, and Rand realized something must have shown in his face.

"Yeah. I was thinking about one friend of mine, when we were in high school. He got tired of Lisa always tagging along, so one day he locked her in a closet so that she couldn't follow us."

"Oh, dear."

"Yeah. Worst part was he forgot to tell anyone. We didn't find her for hours." Rand shook his head. "I'll never forget the look in my parents' eyes when they thought she was truly lost or had been taken."

"What did your friend do?"

"He apologized. My dad somehow kept himself from trouncing the guy, and Lisa said she was okay, she wasn't really scared at all, but we knew better."

"What did you do?"

"Me?" The question surprised him, but after thinking about it a moment he answered, "I found some better friends."

The smile Dorothy gave him then warmed him in the same way his grandmother's approval had once warmed him.

"You remind me so much of my own grandmother," he said, and her smile widened even farther.

"I'll take that as a compliment."

"Do. She was a wonderful lady, and I miss her and my grandfather every day."

"How long since you lost them?" Dorothy asked, her tone sympathetic.

"Two years ago," he said. "Grandpa had a heart attack, and she went less than two days later. She hadn't even been sick, but she didn't want to go on without him."

"I hope Walter and I go together," Dorothy said, in a matter-of-fact tone that told Rand she'd thought about this before. He couldn't imagine ever loving someone that much, but he envied those who had achieved that state.

"How long have you been married?"

"We had our fiftieth last year. Kate threw us a wonderful party. It seemed like the whole town showed up."

"That was nice of her."

"Yes, that's our girl. Always doing things for people. And not just her family, either. Do you know she started a mentor program here in Summer Harbor?"

"Oh?"

"It's done wonders for the kids here. The ones who get in trouble always blame the fact that there's nothing for them to do, so she gave them something."

"That's generous of her."

"She's currently mentoring her second student. The first is already off to college."

"So it's a success, then."

"Oh, yes." Dorothy sighed. "She spends so much of her time on us and everyone else. We worry that she has no life of her own."

"I have a life, thank you."

Dorothy nearly jumped as Kate came up behind them. Rand had heard the footsteps on the stone walkway and wasn't surprised when she appeared.

"My goodness, dear, you startled me!"

"Sorry, Gram." She looked at Rand. "Well, isn't this just too sweet. Run out of things to take snapshots of?"

"Kate!" her grandmother exclaimed, in apparent protest at the sarcasm in her tone. "He's helping me, and it's very kind of him."

"Sorry, Gram," she repeated, but Rand had the feeling she didn't really mean it this time. "Let me change," Kate added, "and I'll join you."

The glance she gave Rand as she went inside was one of undisguised warning.

Well, he thought, *as long as she's suspicious of you, it won't be hard to keep her close enough to watch.*

Not, he added silently with a wry grimace as she returned more quickly than he would have guessed possible, that it would in any way be hard to watch her. Even in the work clothes she apparently kept here, she was lovely.

He thought again of the glamorous photograph he'd seen in the Redstone file. That shot had been taken, he'd guessed by the date on the back, while she was at the high-power, executive position in Denver she'd left to come back here. Here, there was no trace of the designer clothes and careful makeup. She was still lovely, but it was a different kind of beauty, the kind that fit with this place—natural, unaffected. This was a country beauty, not city slickness, and to his surprise Rand found the change refreshing. Perhaps he'd just seen too much in his work around the Redstone world, but he knew quite well that glamour could be a facade that hid something much darker.

Rand was turning some phrasing over in his mind, wondering just how he should approach Kate with questions about the thefts, when her grandmother did it for him.

"Any more problems at work, honey?"

Kate, in the midst of pulling on a pair of gardening gloves, went still. "Gram," she said, with a sideways look at Rand.

"Oh, heavens, child, what do you think Rand's going to do, blab it to the world?"

She looked at him as if she thought that was exactly what he would do. "It's still nothing I want to discuss in front of a total stranger."

There was a sharp undertone in her voice that told him she was beyond just edgy about this. So, did she really just not want to talk about this in front of a stranger—or a *total* stranger as she had emphasized to her grandmother—or was she nervous about something else?

Such as being found out?

Rand stifled a grimace. He really wasn't liking the idea she might be involved. He already liked Dorothy Crawford a great deal, and didn't like to think about what it would do to her to discover such a thing about her granddaughter. It would break her heart. And probably that of crusty Walter Crawford as well, although he'd hide it behind another layer of that gruff exterior.

"I can leave, if you two need to talk," he said neutrally.

Kate had, at least, the grace to blush slightly. "I didn't mean to be rude," she said. "I just try not to discuss company business outside."

"You work for Redstone?"

Her gaze sharpened. "How did you know that?"

He shrugged. "The guy at the gas station mentioned it, when I told him I was staying here."

Dorothy laughed. "Scott Paxton? I can just imagine what he said. In between complaining about the kids at the skateboard park, the way the grocery store is arranged and the color of the sky this morning."

Rand laughed. "That sounds about right."

"He's the local grump, all right," Kate said, smiling now. "Has been ever since he moved here. We try to look on him as entertainment."

It was a lovely smile, Rand noted. And Kate seemed like a good person, a small-town success story of sorts, who had come home to give back to her grandparents and the community. By all Redstone reports she was dedicated and loyal—the sort of person Redstone drew, welcomed and fostered. She was efficient, productive, concerned about the people who worked for her. Exactly the kind of person Josh hunted for.

But she was also used to making a lot more money than she was earning now. Not that Redstone underpaid by any means, the opposite in fact, but she had to have been making very big money in her previous job at that investment firm.

Rand frowned as he dug at the root of what Dorothy had told him was a sprig of Scotch broom, which if left alone would soon overtake the entire garden. What had Kate done with all the money she'd made in that other job? Even if she'd done as many people did and spent it on cars and clothes and a fancy house, there still should have been some left to salvage out of the debris. He'd have to check into that.

The obvious thought hit him then, that her money had gone for another kind of entertainment, the kind that usually went up noses or into veins. He glanced at her now, to where she stood beside her grandmother as they surveyed the garden for the area to tackle next.

Drugs?

He didn't think so. She was tall and toned, not skinny. Her eyes were clear, her nose was tilted sassily upward and not in the least red. And while he wasn't naive enough to think you couldn't find a supply of cocaine even up here in the rural Northwest woods, she didn't have the look. He was no expert, but he'd seen a lot in his years within Redstone security, and she just didn't have the look he'd come to associate with that particular problem.

He'd call Draven. He wouldn't have to mention the possibility, he'd just say he needed to know what her financial situation was, where the big bucks she'd been making had gone. Draven, who said he had been born a cynic and had never found reason to change his mind, would do the rest. He would immediately catch all the possible implications, and if there was anything to be found in Kate Crawford's big-city past, Draven would find it.

And then Rand would have to deal with it.

Chapter 5

"He's absolutely charming, and I don't see why you have such a problem with him."

Kate smothered a sigh. After all the weeding he'd done yesterday she decided it would be best not to say that the first thing she thought of—a snake—when her grandmother said yet again that Rand Singleton was charming. Of course, she was thinking of the man as the snake as well as the charmer, so that completely muddled that metaphor, and she ended up smiling wryly.

"I just worry about you and Gramps. I always have, so don't expect me to stop now."

Dorothy reached across the kitchen table and patted her granddaughter's hand. "We worry about you, too. You really do spend far too much time with us, and not nearly enough living your own life."

Kate sighed audibly this time, drawing a sideways look

from her grandfather from behind his morning newspaper. "She's right," Walter said gruffly, and went back to the sports page, checking, no doubt, for scarce bits of rodeo news. Her grandfather had lived on a ranch in his teens, and had never quite gotten over it.

Kate took a long sip of the coffee her grandmother had poured. In this land of lattes, espresso and more coffee flavors than ice cream flavors, the Crawfords stubbornly stuck to their old, everyday blend. But to Kate it was part of being home.

Her grandmother's worry was an old refrain she'd been hearing since the day she'd come home. It was even why her grandparents had refused to have her move back into this house with them. They insisted she needed her own space and her own life.

"We don't need a keeper yet," Gram had said, and Kate had realized she could easily insult them if she persisted, and that was something she didn't ever want to do.

So she had her own place a couple of miles away, a two-bedroom cottage she had leased from a retired teacher who had moved into a condominium in Seattle. The large master bedroom looked out on a garden with a small pond, while the second bedroom had already been set up as a home office, which made it even more convenient for Kate.

The house sat amid a private stand of tall fir trees and gave her a glimpse of the sound below. She'd put a porch swing in the corner where the view was best, and sat there often regardless of the weather. In fact, one of her favorite things was to be wrapped up in a warm throw in the cold air, listening to the rain on the porch roof and feeling the moisture in the air.

She'd had very little time to do that lately, however. She'd been so distracted by what was happening at Redstone that she'd rarely gotten home before dark. She spent her time trying to solve a mystery, and was missing most of what was turning out to be an incredibly summerlike fall here in the Northwest. They'd barreled through September in the mid-seventies, and October was starting out the same way. She had the feeling they were going to go straight from summer to winter, probably overnight.

She should probably be glad, she thought glumly, that she had the mess at work as a diversion. Otherwise she'd be dwelling on the mess of her life. Obsessing about how badly she'd misjudged the man she'd married. Wondering if she'd ever trust a man again.

And most of all, missing her baby girl.

"Do I smell coffee? Can I beg some?"

Kate went still at the sound of the sleepy, masculine voice behind her. But her grandmother smiled and said a cheery "Good morning, Rand," while her grandfather gestured to the pot and said "Help yourself."

"Thanks."

She didn't turn to look at him. She didn't have to; she could see him perfectly well, reflected in the black, glassy front of the refrigerator. He stretched, expansively, the movement lifting his T-shirt to expose a strip of flat, muscular abdomen above the waistband of his jeans. He ran a hand through his tousled blond hair, yawned, then finally set off toward the coffeemaker.

Kate noticed he knew right where to go for a mug, and for some reason that bothered her. But her feeling of probably selfish perturbation evaporated when he politely brought the carafe over and, when they nodded, refilled both her grandparents' mugs. He then gestured at her with the still half-full pot, but she shook her head and he put it back on the heating plate.

She waited for him to open the fridge for milk, just to further show how at home he'd made himself. But apparently he drank his coffee black because he came back to the table, pulled out a chair and sat. And managed to accomplish it anyway—he did look completely at home.

Not only that, but her grandfather actually put his paper down. Folded it up and set it aside, something she couldn't remember ever seeing while there were parts still unread. She glanced at her grandmother to see how she felt about the fact that this interloper could apparently accomplish with ease what she'd been trying to do for decades. Her grandmother was smiling, so obviously it didn't bother her. Which made it bother Kate all the more.

"Why don't I give you a hand with that gate before I head out, Walt?" the fair-haired boy said.

"I don't want to hold you up," her grandfather protested.

"No problem. I'm not on a set schedule."

"Must be nice," Kate muttered, goaded by his easy familiarity.

"I imagine you always have a set schedule," he said. She tried not to flush; she hadn't really meant to say that loudly enough for him to hear.

"Yes," she said.

"Redstone keeps you busy?"

She gave him a wary, sideways look. "Yes."

"You hear a lot about that company," he said. "What do you think of them?"

"I work in a very small part of Redstone," she said. "But if you mean are they as good to work for as you've heard, yes, they are."

"What exactly is it you do?"

"Distribution."

And that was enough Q and A for her. Her grandparents

may have opened their life books for this man, but she wasn't about to.

"Don't you have pictures to take?" she asked abruptly.

He shifted his gaze to her. He looked at her for a moment, in a steady, assessing way that gave her the awful feeling he thought she was acting like a child. As perhaps she was, jealous of the way he'd beguiled the two people she loved most in the world.

"Eventually," he said easily. "At the moment I'm still looking around."

"Try going out to the lighthouse," her grandfather suggested. "Some good views from there, if you can catch a clear enough day."

"That's the trick," her grandmother put in. "But a clear day here is worth ten days anywhere else, so it's worth waiting for."

So, everybody's delighted with this guy except me, Kate thought as he waved a cheerful goodbye and headed out. Perhaps if she hadn't spent so much time in big cities, she'd be more trusting.

Or gullible, she amended silently.

Not that Gram or Gramps were stupid, not by any stretch. But they were trusting, like many small-town folks. Too trusting, she thought, remembering the boarder who had listened with every evidence of genuine interest and appreciation to her grandparents' suggestions about photos and locations.

He was too good to be real, she thought. And didn't it just figure that the most attractive man she'd seen in ages wasn't just far too young, he was far too charming?

What's she hiding?

Rand had lost count of how many times that question

had popped into his mind yesterday in her grandmother's garden. And again now, as he followed Kate Crawford. There was no doubting she was hiding something. Every time the subject of her work came up while he was around, she either dodged it or changed it immediately. And she did it with that edge that always seemed to appear in her voice and manner on those occasions.

If she was involved, he thought, she needed to work on her poker face.

Maybe that was it. She just acted guilty. But would somebody who had managed to pull off these rather clever thefts really be so awkward about hiding it?

He slowed the rental vehicle as she slowed her nondescript, mud-spattered coupe up ahead. If she was making any sudden and large sums of money, it hadn't turned up in her lifestyle yet. At least, not in her transportation.

It was difficult, in this small town with minimal traffic, to maintain a proper tail. There weren't lanes full of cars to hide among, and there were countless unmarked gravel roads that could be streets or simply driveways for a car you were trying to surreptitiously follow to turn down. And on the often curving roads lined with tall trees, it would be the easiest thing in the world to lose a pursuer, if that were the intent.

But it apparently wasn't Kate's intent, at least not today. Or else she didn't even realize he was behind her. He wasn't sure if that meant she was innocent, or just never expected to be followed. Just how much protection did she think this remote piece of country provided?

He had to swerve wide to avoid three bike riders who insisted on riding side by side, and who in fact cheerfully waved and smiled at him as he went around them, making his irritation seem a bit petty.

When he was safely back in his lane, he had barely enough time to glance down the Redstone driveway and assure himself that she had really made the left turn and gone to work. When he was past it he pulled over, let the bikes he'd just passed go by him again, then made a U-turn. The camera bag on the seat beside him shifted, and he pulled it back as he parked in a turnout behind some large trees a few yards back from the road to Redstone.

It was a spot he'd found in his initial exploration of the area. It didn't seem to belong to anybody, or at least anybody who cared enough to fence it off, so he figured the car would be safe enough. And more important, out of sight.

He opened the camera bag, dug out the camera body and the smaller zoom lens he'd brought. He often used a digital for work, and he'd brought that too, but for this he wanted film. It looked more like the real thing to most people, especially if it was to appear in print as he'd hinted. Besides, he might need the more powerful lens.

When the camera was loaded and ready, he got out and locked the car; no matter how safe this place was, he didn't want to have to deal with the hassle of a burglary with the gun inside or having the rental car stolen. Then he slipped on his small backpack, slung the camera over his shoulder by the contoured strap, grabbed the camera bag and started through the woods. He didn't worry much about encountering anyone; he'd always been amazed at what he could get away with by the simple device of carrying a professional-looking camera. People seemed to expect photographers to be a bit eccentric, and to blithely trek into strange places looking for the perfect shot.

As he was about to blithely trespass onto Redstone property. At least, his undercover persona was about to; as a member of Redstone security, he had open access to any

Redstone facility, but as Rand Singleton, photographer, he could have some explaining to do to keep his cover intact if he was caught.

He made his way through the trees carefully. The ground was already partially obscured by fallen leaves, and on unfamiliar turf it made it difficult to be sure you were stepping down on solid ground. When he was into the woods several yards, he turned to his left and started up the rise. When he'd scouted this place out yesterday, he'd found a perfect spot to set up a surveillance. There was a small break in the trees, giving a view of the towering, rugged Olympic Mountains, a vista well worth photographing.

That the spot also looked straight down on the Redstone plant was, he would insist to anyone who asked, purely coincidence.

Slipping off his pack and setting it and the camera bag down, he stood for a moment, marveling at the view. Those were some very serious mountains, he thought. He'd spent a rough few days in the Andes once, and hiked a long stretch through the Rockies, and these mountains were just as impressive in their own way.

He had to remind himself what he was here for. He dug through his camera gear bag, set up his portable tripod, attached the camera, then aimed it at the most dramatic stretch of rock and glacier he could see. He doubted anyone would spot him up here, but if they did, his story was ready.

Then he opened the backpack and pulled out a small folding tripod-based stool; it wasn't that he didn't want to sit on the ground, but more that the small seat gave him the option to rest his elbows on his knees for support. Something that was going to be necessary soon. Next he took out a pair of ordinary-looking binoculars that were, in fact, quite unusual. A product of Redstone Technologies, they were lightweight but very powerful, wide range, had push-button zoom capability, a range finder with pinpoint accuracy, a remarkable new polarized coating that made it possible to see through glass and water and a stabilizing system that made them easy to use even set for great distances.

But right now they were serving the simple purpose of letting him survey nearly all of the Redstone plant below at once.

Not that there was much to see. The work of the plant was done indoors, and good as the binoculars were, they couldn't help him see through walls. There was the occasional passage of someone from one building to another, and vehicles came and went from the outside, but mostly it was quiet. This whole place was quiet, he thought.

Once, he saw Kate come out of the main building and walk quickly across to the manufacturing building, where he could see several vehicles parked, including two of the bobtail trucks used to move product out from this production center. He hadn't had his eyes to the binoculars at that moment, but nevertheless he knew it was her. He could tell not only by the dark, shiny fall of hair that swung as she went, but by the very way she walked, with that long-legged grace he'd noticed in her the first time he'd ever seen her move.

She was in the manufacturing building for nearly twenty minutes, and when she came out she was walking more slowly, as if thinking about something. Halfway across the courtyard that was landscaped to look almost like the untouched land surrounding the facility, she picked up speed again and went back to the main building where he knew her office was. He settled back down to watch some more, not sure what he was waiting to see, only that he would know it when he did.

By noon he was glad of the sandwich Dorothy had insisted he take with him. He opened the bottle of water he'd brought and took a bite of the thick stack of ham, cheese, tomato and some nicely spicy mustard on slices of bread so fresh he wondered if she'd baked it herself. It wouldn't surprise him after the incredible stuffed pork chops she'd insisted he join her and Walter for last night.

I'll have to add board to the room rent, he thought idly, shifting his glance once more to the mountains to the west. Amazing to see all this salt water around, yet know the actual ocean was on the other side of those towering peaks. This was truly a magical place. From everything he'd seen, life seemed slower, easier and much more sane than he was used to. He could see where it would grow on a person. And why Josh so loved it here that he'd sited this wing of Redstone in this place.

Even Kate's life seemed simple and clean here, he thought as he walked back to the camera, figuring he'd better have some actual shots to show, to prove he was for real. She went to work, she spent lots of time with the people she loved, she breathed clean air, she glowed with health, appreciated the loveliness around her, she—

He snapped out of the uncharacteristic reverie as an oddly furtive motion from below drew his attention. A young woman, a girl really, had come out the same door Kate had, but she had turned and headed toward the small car parking area. She was walking oddly, hunched over, holding a sweater that looked too big for her closed in front with both hands as if it were much colder out than it actually was. That distracted him for the moment from the maroon-tinted hair that told him Summer Harbor was perhaps not so isolated from the rest of the world after all.

The girl walked quickly to an old blue sedan with oxidized paint. She fumbled with a set of keys, dropped them, clutched the sweater tighter as she bent to pick them up. She finally got the trunk open. She leaned over, slid something out from under the sweater and into the trunk. She backed up hastily and slammed the truck lid closed.

She turned and ran back to the building.

Rand clicked off the last shot of the girl that would be recognizable, took his finger off the shutter release, and began to think about where to have some film developed.

And to wonder if he'd already found the thief.

Chapter 6

"I was just about convinced I'd slipped back in time here," Rand said as he leaned into the shovel. "Then I saw a girl with maroon hair."

Dorothy laughed. "Melissa Morris. She's actually Kate's new mentee, I guess you call it. You should have seen her before she started the program—it was blue."

So she was even younger than he'd thought. He got a sick feeling in his gut as the idea that Kate had recruited this girl to help in the thefts occurred to him. At least he told himself that's what it was, that it wasn't just the idea of Kate being involved herself.

"Deep enough?" he asked, gesturing at the irregular six by six hole he'd dug.

He'd come out this morning to find Dorothy trying to do this herself. He'd stopped and asked her about it, and she'd explained she wanted it done before Walt came back from the barber, so he wouldn't feel compelled to volunteer to do it despite his knees.

Dorothy had also made it clear she didn't want him to feel compelled either, but he'd talked her into letting him take over anyway.

Dorothy leaned over now to inspect the depth of her new bulb bed. "I need about another two inches, if you don't mind. The daffodils need to be deeper."

"No problem," he said, and hefted the shovel again before continuing the conversation. "Did Kate choose her?"

"Melissa? Actually, it was the other way around. She wanted to work with Kate. Asked for her specifically, or I doubt Kate would have taken her on."

"Is she a problem?"

"She's been in a little trouble. Nothing serious, just kid stuff." She gave a little chuckle. "But what's serious out here would be kid stuff in the city."

Like theft? Rand wondered. Was that why Kate had agreed to take on a problem child, did she figure it would be easy to involve the kid?

Don't get carried away. You're making her sound like Fagan, or whatever that guy's name in Oliver Twist *was,* he told himself.

"Melissa would be fine," Dorothy said, "if it wasn't for that boyfriend of hers. Now there's trouble."

"Oh?"

"You mark my words, one day we're going to open the paper and see Derek Simon's photo on page one, and it won't be for anything good."

"So…he's a bad influence?"

"You never would have seen her with that hair before," Dorothy said. "But I tell myself it's no different than the bobs women got in the twenties. They were shocking then, and this is now, which is the point at that age, I suppose."

Rand smiled at her. "It's a tough age. I remember following a few trends in high school that make me cringe now."

"Funny how they think they're being so unique, yet end up all looking alike, isn't it?"

He laughed at that, unable to deny the simple truth of what she'd said. "You sure you don't want me to help with the rest of this?" he asked, gesturing at the hole he'd dug.

"Oh, no, thank you dear. The rest is sheer pleasure for me, mixing in the bone meal and compost, and planting the bulbs. You just leave the soil there in the wheelbarrow, and I'll do the rest."

"If you're sure," he said. "I don't mind. My mom tries every year to grow bulbs, but she hasn't quite got the knack of it down in Southern California."

"Tell her she should try planting ranunculus, and sparaxis. They're considered bulbs, and they do well down there, I think. Lovely flowers, too."

"I'll tell her that."

"You tell her to call me if she wants to talk about it. And thank you again, Rand. This was very sweet of you."

"No," he said, meaning it. "It was good of you to let me help. I'm never in one place long enough to even think about a garden."

"So, it keeps you trotting around the globe, your photography work?"

"I travel a lot," he said; that at least wasn't a lie. He tried to avoid direct lies whenever possible. "Speaking of which, if you're sure you don't need me, I guess I'd better get started."

"Oh, dear, I shouldn't have kept you from—"

She stopped when Rand held up a hand. "Please, I mean it, I was glad to do it."

"Walt can't do this like he used to. His knees are just too bad. But he would have tried, and maybe hurt himself, so I truly thank you."

"Has he considered replacement? My grandfather did it, said it was the best thing he'd ever done."

"We've considered it," Dorothy said, but she didn't look at him when she said it. Nor did she say anything more on the subject.

He thought about that as he loaded his photography gear into the car, and then headed out. He wondered if those bills he'd seen were what was stopping them. He frowned at the idea. No wonder Walt was gruff; he could well be hiding a lot of pain and frustration behind that crotchety exterior. Just like Dorothy was hiding a lot of worry and strain behind her cheerful demeanor.

He was surprised at how much both ideas bothered him. He *liked* the Crawfords, and the idea that they might be doing without anything—let alone needed medical treatment—grated on him. He put it on his mental list of things to look into. Right behind the whereabouts of Kate's former income, an inquiry he had yet to make. He wasn't sure why he was putting it off, but he knew that he was. He told himself it was because he was still just getting started on this case, but even he didn't quite believe that.

His surveillance today took a different turn. Shortly after noon, Kate came out of the main, lodge-style building and walked to her car. There was no sign of the furtiveness he'd seen in the maroon-haired girl, but it was a change in the pattern he'd seen since he'd been here, so it caught his attention.

Lunch? he wondered with a glance at his watch. Possi-

bly. Maybe the post office, although she hadn't been carrying anything. Could be in her purse, or briefcase, whatever that bag thing was she had slung over her shoulder.
Heck, anything could be in there.

He wondered if it was a holdover from her big-city
days, where women often carried a pair of walking shoes
to travel between a subway station and their office, where
they then changed into dress shoes. Or maybe she was just
one of those that had to have a ton of stuff with them all
the time; he'd never understood that. But it seemed to be
the norm; his frequent partner, Samantha Beckett—Samantha Gamble now, he corrected himself—had been the
only woman he'd ever known who preferred to carry no
purse at all.

It suddenly occurred to him how small the insulin
pumps were. And that it would be easy to carry several of
them in a bag that size.

Could it be that simple? Was she simply walking out
with them, in plain view of everyone?

*The more complicated the plan, the bigger the chance
for failure.*

Rand tried to remember. Had it been Draven who had
said it? No…St. John. It had been Josh's mysterious right-
hand man who had said it, but Draven had agreed, in the
more blunt terms of Keep It Simple, Stupid. Whenever
one of them came up with some elaborate plan for a job,
he always found a way to simplify it, telling them to leave
the *Mission Impossible* schemes to Hollywood.

Simple. What could be simpler than sticking a few
things in your big purse and walking out the door, the same
way you did every day? Were the boxes that were found
empty at the delivery point in fact empty when they went
into the truck in the first place? Was that why there was no

sign of damage on the truck's locks, because in fact the trucks had never been broken into?

Suddenly where Kate was headed became critical. He waited until she opened the driver's door and got in, and he heard the car start. When it was clear she was actually going to leave, he grabbed up his equipment hastily and headed down the path to his car at a run.

He tossed the camera and binoculars somewhat haphazardly into the front seat, jumped in, then started the rental and maneuvered back toward the road. Her blue coupe was nowhere in sight. He inched forward, until he could see both ways down the road. He was just in time to catch a flash of blue headed toward town.

"Such as it is," he muttered as he turned that direction, at the same time being thankful there was so little traffic that he didn't lose her.

She turned into the small shopping center that held the post office, the sandwich shop and the Curl and Cut.

The post office? he wondered. Was she actually mailing the things through the U.S. Mail? You couldn't get much more basic than that. Draven and St. John would appreciate the simplicity of it.

She parked at the outer edge of the parking lot, although there were several spaces available closer in. Odd, he thought. He pulled into the lot, stopping several yards away in the shelter of a huge four-by-four pickup. He watched as she got out of her car, waited to see where she was headed. If she indeed went to the post office, he wasn't sure what he would do. Come up with some story to get the clerk to tell him where the package had been sent. Maybe something about Kate sending him, afraid she'd put the wrong zip code on it or something. Or maybe—

She went into the sandwich shop. It was small, and even

from here he could see the edge of the counter, where a couple of people stood waiting. She walked up to the end of the short line, her head tilted back, apparently studying the overhead menu.

Lunch.

He let out a long breath that warned him he was way too tense about this. He'd been right the first time, before his imagination had run riot on him. Or maybe she was just going to eat first, mail later.

That didn't seem likely. Who'd sit around with hot property burning a hole in their pocket—or purse—when they could simply be rid of it so easily, two doors down? The longer she lugged the stuff around, the more chance there was she'd get caught with it. Of course, who outside of Redstone would even realize? She worked there, after all, so why shouldn't she have Redstone property?

Rand sighed. Why was what should have been a simple theft investigation getting so complicated? Maybe he should have gone in on the inside, it would have been easier.

But his gut told him it also would have been less effective. She—or whoever the thief was—might have gotten suspicious of any new personnel coming in. It wasn't likely they would know him as security; they kept a very low profile whenever possible. But any changes tended to make thieves nervous. Guilt made them inclined to see everything that happened in relation to what they were doing, even if it had no connection at all. Even if it was something as simple as a new employee. Especially in a small facility like this one.

And that nervousness might make them shut down operations entirely. Which would, admittedly, solve the theft problem. But Josh wanted whoever was responsible for this, and he wanted them badly.

Rand had rarely seen the big boss angry, but when it happened, it was enough to make the most dangerous of opponents think twice. There was a long history of has-beens who were has-beens because they'd underestimated the brilliance, tenacity, passion and vision of the lanky, gray-eyed man with the lazy drawl. That tendency of many to see only the surface, the easygoing manner, the quiet demeanor, the tinge of the many places he'd lived in his voice, and then judge him as a bit naive, maybe even slow, was one of Josh's greatest strengths. He knew it, and used it without qualm; the fault was on the side of those who failed to look beyond the surface. Anyone who thought he'd stumbled into his wealth, or had built his empire on the backs of underlings or through dumb luck, paid the price such ignorance and presumption deserved.

Rand watched as, now with a sandwich and a mug of soup on a tray, Kate moved to one of the small tables by the door. When she set the tray down and slipped her bag off her shoulder, clearly intending to stay and eat, Rand got out of his car. He considered the gun, but since he wasn't about to use it in this very public and busy place, he left it. He kept his eyes on her as he walked toward the shop. She took something out of the bag, what looked like a PDA. She tapped it a couple of times with the stylus, then propped it up on the bag and picked up her sandwich as she looked at the small screen, apparently not relaxing even now.

She never even looked up when he came in, hardly the actions of someone with a load of stolen goods on them. But the bag was close at hand, and removing the PDA didn't appear to have taken down the volume any.

He decided quickly to grab a chance.

"Hey, Kate, hi!" he called, making a sharp turn as if he'd just spotted her. In his movement he caught the edge of the table with his leg, sending her bag sliding. "Uh-oh," he said, reaching as if to catch it, but in fact making sure it went over the edge.

Her sharp exclamation of surprise and concern echoed in his ears. Was it normal for the situation? He wasn't sure, but she didn't sound panicked, or afraid, not even when he apologized profusely and knelt to gather the bag—and get a glimpse of what was in it.

He saw a wallet, a flip-up cell phone, a small zippered nylon bag, several pens and a notebook—apparently she didn't completely trust the PDA—a thick paperback book, and what was taking up most of the room, a clipboard holding several papers.

She could be hiding something in the zippered bag, he supposed, but he'd seen a sample of the packaged pump, and if she could get more than a couple in there, he'd be surprised. And they were disappearing by the dozen.

Of course, she could be getting ready to make contact with a new customer, perhaps just bringing a sample to convince them she really had access to the pumps.

And maybe she just came out to get some lunch, he muttered inwardly as he set the bag back on the table.

"I'm sorry," he repeated. "I just didn't expect to see you here."

"Sooner or later everyone in Summer Harbor ends up here," she said.

"I didn't break anything, did I?" he asked, gesturing at the bag.

"I already had out the only thing that could break," she said, gesturing at the PDA.

"Whew," he said, "I'm glad." He gestured at her lunch tray. "So, is the food good here, or are they just the only thing around?"

She studied him for a moment, as if she were trying to decide if there had been an insult to her beloved Summer Harbor in his question. Whatever she decided, she answered evenly enough.

"Both."

"What do you recommend?"

"Depends on your taste. And how much time you've got. The French onion soup is wonderful, but it takes a while to eat. Their hot chicken sandwich is great."

He nodded, glanced at the counter and saw they were clear, and figured he could get his order and come back here before she finished. Unless he'd scared her off and she sped through the rest of her meal.

Deciding it would seem too odd if he didn't order the lunch he'd supposedly come in here for, he walked over and asked for the recommended sandwich. When he had it, he walked back to her table as quickly as he could manage without looking like he was rushing.

"Do you mind?" he asked, gesturing at the empty seat opposite her, and then pulling it out to sit before she really had a chance to answer. "I decided on just a sandwich. I'll save the soup until it gets really cold."

She lifted one dark, sleek brow at him. "You plan on being here that long?"

"I like it here," he said, and found somewhat to his surprise that it was nothing less than the truth. "The people are really nice."

"Yes, they are," she said. "Nice, and generous and… trusting."

He didn't miss the slight emphasis on the last word. What he didn't know was what it meant. Was it an unconscious thing, stemming from her ability to fool those trusting people she was talking about? Or did she put herself in that category as well, implying that her innocent trust resulted in the current mess at Redstone?

He hadn't thought about that aspect, really. If she was innocent, then she was in a very difficult place, being responsible for the shipping of the product, and the fact that the thefts were apparently occurring in her jurisdiction, as it were.

But he still thought she was awfully edgy for an innocent person.

So much for her quiet, peaceful lunch, Kate thought. She hadn't realized how much she'd been looking forward to it until the too charming Mr. Singleton had interrupted. He'd nearly startled her out of her chair when he'd knocked her bag off the table. He'd been nice about it, though, retrieving it for her and being so concerned that he'd broken something. But now he didn't seem disposed to leave and let her return to her meal in peace.

"Your grandmother seems pretty worried," he said, startling her again.

"Excuse me?"

"She seems worried. I know part of it is about your grandfather, and his knees, but is there something else bothering her as well?"

"Nothing you need to worry about," she said, instantly on guard at the personal question.

He didn't take the hint. "I noticed she seemed upset at the mail, some bills that came."

Anger kicked through her. *You want to know if you're wasting your time? If they have enough money to make them worth ripping off?*

"I don't know anyone who likes bills coming in," she said, stalling as her mind raced. Should she lie and say they were dead broke, so he would go poach elsewhere? But wasn't it clear they weren't rich from the fact that they were renting out their own room to a total stranger? And besides, the idea of just driving him away to prey on someone else didn't sit well with her.

"I was just wondering," he said, as if he realized he'd betrayed too much.

"Do you always get so involved with total strangers?" she asked, unable to quite suppress the edge that came into her voice.

He studied her for a moment, as if he were analyzing her tone as much as what she had said. "I like them," he finally said.

And you're making sure they like you, she thought, that anger stirring anew.

"They remind me of my own grandparents."

"Oh?" She left it at that, wanting to see what he'd say, how far he'd go with this ploy.

"Yes, they do. My grandmother especially. She was a lot like yours."

He looked wistful. Kate stopped herself from asking about that past-tense reference, telling herself this was just his way of further charming her vulnerable grandparents and trying to win points with her. Well, it wasn't going to work on her.

"Taken any good pictures yet?" She kept the sarcasm to a minimum; whatever he was up to, she didn't want to scare him off before she found out.

"Won't know that 'til I get them developed. But if not, it's surely my fault. I've got good equipment and the material's all here."

The modest admission surprised her a little. But then she told herself it was all part of the act, the same practiced dispensing of charm that had her grandparents practically ready to adopt him.

"You're a bit late for the height of the fall color." *And wouldn't a real photographer have known that?*

"I know. But actually, the bare branches of the deciduous trees set against the backdrop of the evergreens fascinates me more. It's almost sculptural. Especially the madronas, with that red bark."

Kate blinked. For a con man, that was a rather artistic-sounding statement to make. And he'd said it with an enthusiasm she found hard to disbelieve. She found herself wondering again if maybe he was for real.

That's why they call them con men, she told herself. *Don't you go falling for the act!*

She focused on her sandwich as if finishing it were the most important thing in the world. And as if chewing carefully enough could somehow keep her from succumbing to that charm that had her grandparents so bewitched. When that didn't work, she sipped at her soda as if it could give her immunity to his polished act. Problem was, it didn't seem to be working. How could a man she didn't trust, in fact was very suspicious of, make her pulse kick into high speed like this? How could she heat up at the sight of him when she was afraid he might harm her grandparents? She'd never been betrayed by her body before, but that's what this felt like. It was as if her senses had suddenly refused to listen to her brain, and she didn't like the confusion.

She was still telling herself it was an act as she drove back to the office. And as she spent the afternoon on the spreadsheet Mel had needed, working on closing it out for the third quarter, it took her much longer than it should have, because her thoughts kept straying to a pair of blue eyes that seemed too open and honest to hide what she suspected he was hiding.

She told herself it had nothing to do with his unquestionable appeal. She was simply worried about the way he was worming his way so deeply into her grandparents' lives so quickly, and how she was going to protect them while still keeping a handle on this theft situation at work. She told herself all of that, then repeated it.

It didn't help much.

"You've got to *get* a handle on it before you can *keep* a handle on it," she muttered to the screen she'd been staring at for who knew how long now.

When *at last* the phone rang, she welcomed the interruption. A glance at the clock told her it was nearly time to get out of here anyway. Quickly she saved her work and shut down the spreadsheet program, then swiveled her chair back to the desk to pick up the phone.

"Katy, you'll never believe it," her grandmother said, obviously excited about something.

"Believe what, Gram?"

"It's so exciting! I got a phone call this afternoon from a man, about some money."

"Money? What money?"

"I'm trying to tell you, dear. He talked so fast it was hard to keep up, but he was going on and on about this money that was sitting in an account that he couldn't get to, but we could. He said all we had to do was put up the same amount, to show good faith, and—"

"You haven't done anything?" she exclaimed.

"Well no, we only called the man back to set up a meeting. Rand said we should—"

A chill went through her. "Rand told you to call this guy back?"

"Yes, he said we should go along with the plan, then we could—"

"I'm on my way. Don't do anything, *anything* until I get there," Kate snapped.

She slammed down the phone. Singleton's con had begun.

She broke the speed limit every mile of the way, her heart hammering. She was a fool. She should never have let this go this far. She should have thrown him out the moment she laid eyes on him.

Her tires threw up a spray of gravel as she made a rapid turn down her grandparents' driveway. She scrambled out of her car the instant it came to a stop. Left the door standing open. Ran to the house.

Moments later she was back standing on the front porch, dread clenching around her heart painfully. A glance through the garage window only heightened her fears. Their tired old station wagon was inside.

But her grandparents—and Rand Singleton's car— were gone.

Chapter 7

It had never occurred to her to program the sheriff's department number into her cell phone. Her life here just didn't require that. Or so she'd thought. Around here, for the most part, people either called 911 or handled it themselves. A life-or-death emergency you called for help on, anything else you just took care of yourself.

She ran back to her car, although she wasn't sure exactly where she was going to go. She dug out her cell phone as she started the engine and headed back out the driveway. Summer Harbor wasn't that big, and she could search it fairly thoroughly in a short time, but she had no idea if they were even still in town. Of course, they couldn't have gotten far in the few minutes since she'd left Redstone, but if Singleton had taken them out of town…

Damn it, she thought as she began the process of dialing information and getting the sheriff's nonemergency

number from her cell service, she was going to get them a
cell phone, whether they wanted it or not. And make them
learn how to use it.

It suddenly occurred to her that her grandparents could
well be in actual danger. Didn't that warrant a call to 911?
She obviously wasn't thinking clearly. She disconnected
and made the three-digit call as she turned back onto the
main highway.

What she hadn't realized was that 911 calls from a cell
phone went to a central communications office, not the
more local one, and it took an extra few seconds for the
dispatcher to work out exactly where she was. And in that
time, she made a discovery.

Singleton's rented SUV was parked in front of, of all
places, the Curl and Cut.

She dropped her cell and yanked the steering wheel,
barely making the turn into the parking lot in front of a delivery van that pulled out from the bank drive-through. As
soon as it was safe she grabbed the phone, told the dispatcher to cancel for now, she'd call back, and disconnected.

She parked behind Singleton's vehicle, effectively
blocking him in. Then she got out and ran toward the Curl
and Cut's door.

She slowed when she got a look through the big window in front. Through the ornately painted *C* of Curl, she
saw a group of people huddled in the back half of the
salon. Among them were her grandparents, Esther, Cheryl
from the sandwich shop and Rand Singleton. And they
were all looking toward her.

No, she realized, coming to a halt now. They weren't
looking at her. They were looking at the bank.

She glanced over her shoulder, but saw nothing unusual at the small, shingle-sided building. Frowning she

turned back to the salon door she was now standing in front of.

Singleton was there, pulling the door open and gesturing her inside. "Come on," he said, his tone just short of being an order. "Get inside, like you had an appointment."

She hesitated for a moment, but only a moment; her grandparents were in here, so even if this was some sort of crazy hostage situation, this was where she had to be.

"Come in, Kate!" her grandmother called out.

"I called the sheriff," she warned Singleton as she stepped inside. "They're on the way." No need, she decided, to tell him she'd cancelled the call.

"They're already here," he said.

She blinked. "What?"

"They're already here," he repeated. "We're just waiting."

"Waiting for what?"

"For the arrest!" Her grandmother had come up to them, the smile on her face wide with excitement. "I tried to tell you, but you were so brusque on the phone."

"Arrest?" she asked, feeling more than a little stupid.

"It worked exactly like Rand said it would," her grandfather put in. "We played along, just like he told us to."

Her grandmother actually giggled. "We acted like we were too silly to realize it was a swindle, and they bought it!"

"Teach them to think gray hair means gray thinking," her grandfather said.

"There! There they come," Esther yelped, pointing.

Kate turned along with everyone else. At the bank, three people were coming out. A man, flanked closely by another man in a sheriff's uniform and an older woman with white hair in a tidy bun, wearing a flowered dress that looked vaguely familiar to Kate.

A woman who didn't move like an older woman at all.

"Yes!" Kate's grandfather exclaimed. "We caught him!"

Kate watched, a little stunned, as the trio turned and walked toward a plain, dark green car parked beside the bank. The man in the center was put in the back seat, and only then did Kate see that he was handcuffed. The woman closed the door, checked the lock, then walked to the front passenger door of a second green vehicle parked next to the first. She unlocked it and tossed the handbag she'd been clutching inside. Then she reached up to her head. With a couple of tugs the white hair came off. The female officer shook her head and then ran her fingers through a short crop of sandy brown hair.

"Remember my Halloween wig?" her grandmother asked. "And that's my old housedress she's wearing."

Kate turned to stare at Dorothy Crawford. "What," she said, "happened?"

"It was Rand's idea. First he called the sheriff, and they worked it out."

Rand had called the sheriff? The man she'd suspected all along had in fact called the cops?

"Worked what out?" Kate ask, hanging on to her patience.

"How to set 'em up," her grandfather said, chuckling. "Rand told us exactly how to string the guy along, convince him we were really going to meet him here at the bank and hand over ten thousand dollars."

"All I did was call the sheriff. Dorothy did the real work," Rand said. "She played her part perfectly."

Was this for real? Kate wondered. *Or was it all part of a plan to gain her grandparents' confidence? No, surely it wasn't worth somebody getting arrested for, there were too many easier marks out there.*

She shook her head sharply, trying to clear it. She wasn't sure what she thought anymore. It wasn't that she couldn't accept that she might have been wrong about Rand, but she couldn't help still being suspicious.

Maybe you have *spent too much time in big cities,* she thought. Probably almost everybody in Summer Harbor would take Rand Singleton at face value. Maybe even she would have, if she hadn't been so worried about Gram and Gramps. But when it came to the two people she loved most in the world, she couldn't take any chances.

When she learned the sheriff needed her grandparents to give a report, she automatically assumed she would take them. But the female officer cheerfully offered not only to give them a ride but bring her, and the borrowed dress, back home when they were done. This was her favorite kind of arrest, she told them, since her own dearest aunt had once been victimized by slime like this. Her grandparents excitedly accepted, and Kate didn't have the heart to interfere.

"Good," Rand said. "I'll take Kate out and feed her, to make up for missing out on most of the excitement."

"What?" she almost yelped.

"Wonderful!" her grandmother exclaimed. "Go to the Italian place, across from the marina. Kate loves it."

They were gone before she could put together a coherent protest. And Rand was unlocking his rental's passenger door as if it were a given she was indeed going with him.

"We'll come back for your car later. I'll move it over for you so I can get out," he said. "Do you think Esther will mind if you leave it here for a couple of hours?"

"No," she said, distracted from her intention to refuse to go by the question, and feeling a bit silly for having blocked him in, even though he hadn't said a word about it. He quickly reparked her car and came back.

"Let's go," he said, pulling open the passenger door. "You're lucky I had to clean this out for your grandparents. I'm afraid I tend to toss things when I'm working."

"You toss cameras?"

He grinned. It was mouthwatering. *He* was mouthwatering. She smothered a sigh as he answered her.

"Film canisters mostly. And boxes. Food wrappers. Soda cans. I'm a slob, but only temporarily. I clean it out every night, honest."

In that moment, with that grin and that self-deprecating explanation, she lost the battle she'd been fighting. And when he held the door open for her, she got in.

It's only dinner, she told herself.

He drove directly to the restaurant, so she supposed he'd seen it before. When the waiter—Mel's older brother, Mike—approached and asked if they wanted a drink, Kate hesitated. She liked the thought of a relaxing glass of wine after the ups and downs of the day, but she couldn't help thinking she'd be better off with all her wits about her to deal with this man. And that was just mentally. Physically, she wasn't sure her wits would be much help. She hadn't felt this way around a man for a very long time, and she was out of practice dealing with it. In the end she declined and asked for water. Rand ordered, on Mike's recommendation, a beer from a local microbrewery.

Perusing the menu—although Kate wondered why she bothered, since she almost always had their amazing shrimp scampi—took more time, but once Mike had returned and taken their orders, they were left with no choice but to talk or pointedly avoid speaking to each other. Obviously Rand felt no desire to avoid conversation, because he chatted away easily, about harmless things. And because it was easier—and because she still felt chagrinned at how wrong she'd apparently been about him—she participated.

"It hasn't rained since I've been here," he said. "Was I misled about the Northwest's famous weather?"

"You mean infamous, don't you?"

"Maybe," he agreed with that grin she'd already decided was deadly.

"No, you weren't misled. It can rain here for days, even weeks on end. But I find it a small price to pay for the beauty. Besides, I love the rain."

"You don't get tired of it?"

"No. I get tired of summer, days on end without rain," she said.

"Did you miss it when you were off working in Denver?"

"Yes, I did," she answered.

"Is that why you came home?"

"Partly." She was beginning to feel a bit pressured by the string of questions.

"That, and to work for Redstone?"

He seemed inordinately interested in Redstone, and that also made her nervous. "Partly," she repeated.

He studied her for a moment before saying softly, "But mostly for your grandparents."

It wasn't a question, so she didn't answer, merely shrugged.

He leaned back in the colorful upholstered booth. "You know, most people tend to trust me."

"I'm sure they do," she said, still feeling edgy. "But some of us require more than a pretty face."

He blinked. "You know, if I dissect that completely and ignore the implied insult, I think I might be able to find a compliment in there."

Kate winced inwardly. It *had* been insulting, in a way.

And she wasn't usually that kind of person. And she chose to ignore the compliment remark; he had to know what he looked like, and what effect it had. Finally she resorted to a somewhat lame, "I'm sorry. I'm still a little wound up, I guess."

"Are you apologizing for the insult or the compliment?"

Her gaze shot up to his face. She saw the glint of humor in his eyes, and suddenly she realized the other part of why she was so edgy. She owed him another apology. One that was going to be much more unpleasant.

No point putting it off, she told herself, and plunged ahead. "I owe you a much bigger apology."

He lifted a brow. "For?"

She should have thought more about how she was going to word this. "I'm very protective of my grandparents," she began.

"I noticed." His mouth twisted wryly when he said it, but his tone was gentle.

"When you first moved in, I thought…I was sure…."

"That I was after something from them?" he suggested. "Their life savings, the house maybe?"

"I just couldn't see why somebody like you would want to stay with people their age, in a tiny place like this."

"Somebody like me." He sat back in the booth, again studying her for a long silent moment. She could almost see him processing, remembering. "Today," he said finally, "you thought I was in on it, didn't you?"

"Yes," she said, startled that she sounded almost defiant. What was wrong with her, reacting like this when she'd meant only to apologize?

"In fact," he said thoughtfully, watching her, "you thought I was up to something like that pigeon drop scam from the beginning, didn't you?"

She didn't try to deny it. "Yes, I did."

"You made a lot of assumptions about me in a big hurry."

She couldn't deny the truth of that, either. "Yes." She lifted her gaze to his face. Met those too-beautiful blue eyes. "For that I apologize, but somehow I don't think I'm the first one to make assumptions based on your looks."

For an instant he looked startled, but then a slow smile curved his mouth. "No. No, you're not. But I confess, I've apparently been spoiled. Usually those assumptions are…more positive."

That smile was so open, so engaging, that she couldn't help smiling back. She no longer doubted her grandparents assessment of him. He really was a nice guy. She quickly buried the realization that the fact made him more dangerous to her equilibrium.

"I'm sure they are," she said. "It's just me, Rand, really."

"You love them very much," he said simply, graciously, as if that were the only explanation needed. That made her feel another pang of guilt that she had misjudged him.

"They raised me, you know. After my parents took off to wander the world and never came back."

He drew back slightly. "Took off? I got the idea they had died, many years ago."

She grimaced. "They might as well have. They decided when I was ten that they weren't cut out to live an average life. Started asking how anybody could exist without knowing who they really were."

"Sounds a bit…"

"Immature? Selfish? In the throes of a midlife crisis?" she suggested, hating that after all this time she could still sound bitter.

"All of the above," Rand said. "I can't even imagine. My

folks are so grounded. They're the rock we're all built on. Me, my sister, even my aunts, uncles and cousins gather around them."

With that simple, heartfelt declaration, he managed to erase any lingering reservations she'd had about him.

"They sound wonderful," she said.

"They are. Of course, I didn't appreciate it for a long time. It was ama zing how much they learned while I was in college."

She laughed. He sounded so…normal. So open and honest. She felt foolish for ever having suspected him of anything nefarious.

"I think your grandparents would like them," he said.

"I'm sure they would. It might hurt them, though."

He gave her a quizzical look. "Why?"

"They're still trying to figure out where they went wrong with my parents."

"Ah. Parental Guilt Complex."

"Is that what it is?"

"That's what my mom calls it. That quirk parents have that makes them forget all about free will and the million outside influences and decide that they're responsible for everything their kid ever does."

Kate found herself laughing again. It felt good, noticeably, and she wondered how long it had been since she'd really laughed.

Probably since the first theft, she answered herself silently. And while that problem certainly hadn't gone away, it was a relief not to have worry about her grandparents piled on top of it.

"Do you have any contact with your parents at all?" he asked.

"Not in several months. But that's not unusual. They're down to calling about once a year, and I think they only do it then to let us know they are still alive."

Rand shook his head. "Once a year? That's it? To their only daughter?"

"It used to be more. When I was a kid, I'd get a birthday gift from some off-the-wall place, and the occasional postcard. But once I hit eighteen, that stopped."

"Like they'd shed the last bit of responsibility, now that you were legally an adult?"

Kate drew back slightly, startled. "That's exactly what I thought. It was as if they'd been waiting all that time with that one last thread holding them back, and they were finally able to cut it."

He shook his head again. "I can't imagine. If I hadn't had my parents to turn to, even when I was mad at them, I don't know what I would have done. How I would have turned out. Certainly not as well as you have."

Kate fought the blush she felt trying to heat her cheeks. *It was just a simple compliment,* she told herself. *Don't react like a teenager.*

"I had Gram and Gramps," she said. "After my parents left we became a family. We had each other, so we barely missed them."

Rand studied her once more before saying, "And you've spent your life trying to make up to your grandparents for what your parents did."

She stared at him. "What?"

"You've made sure you were the kind of child they should have had, haven't you?"

She'd never thought about it in quite that way, and it stunned her that this man she barely knew—and who barely knew her—had seen it. There was, apparently, a lot more to Rand Singleton than met the eye.

Pleasing as what met the eye was.

By the time dinner arrived, Kate was very much afraid she was well on the way to being as charmed by him as her grandparents were.

Chapter 8

"Melissa Moore and Derek Simon," Rand said into the phone. "They're high school kids, juveniles, but get what you can. I'm guessing they're both sixteen."

"Got it. Urgent?"

"No. Not yet."

"Next?"

Rand's mouth quirked upward. Conversations with Draven were always challenging, but never lengthy. His half smile faded as he realized what the next thing on his mental list was, and how reluctant he was to look behind the door this inquiry might open.

But he had to do it. He'd begun to both like and admire Kate for her devotion to her family and his love for this small community, but that didn't—couldn't—matter. It was part of the job, it was an obvious question, and if he didn't ask it they were going to start wondering. Just because he might not like the answer he got didn't change the fact that he had to ask the question. He'd put it off long enough.

"Kate Crawford," he said, not realizing until he said it how grim he was going to sound. He tried for a more casual tone. "I want to know where all that high salary went when she was working for Funding International in Denver."

"Oh?"

"She seems to be on a short financial string. She had to be making good money for those years she was playing with the big boys, so I want to know why things are so tight now."

"All right. Rush?"

"No. Thorough's more important."

"Take a while then."

"And run me a Scott Paxton. He's about fifty, I'd guess. Apparently hasn't been here all that long."

"Suspect?"

"Maybe. Works at the gas station. Mad at the world, apparently including Redstone."

It wasn't until after he hung up that Rand realized how few places he'd spent any time in where you could say *the* gas station and everyone would know where you meant. The novelty of this place still hadn't worn off. He was beginning to think it never would.

Not that he was going to be staying long enough for that to be an issue, of course.

He sat thinking for a moment, in this room that had once been Dorothy and Walt Crawford's. The room Walt could no longer climb the stairs to get to. Then he picked up his cell phone again and pushed another speed dial button. It rang twice before a woman answered.

"Sam?"

"Hey, what's up? I thought you were in the north woods somewhere."

Samantha Gamble's voice was light and cheerful, as it had been with steady regularity since her marriage to Redstone's resident genius, Ian Gamble. They were a pair no one in their right mind would think would work, yet they did; they were one of the happiest couples Rand had ever seen.

"I am. I need some info."

"Whatever I can do, you know that."

"Actually, not you. Ian."

"Oh." If Sam was startled, it didn't show. "Well, he's right here. Hang on."

A few moments later her husband was there, and he wasn't as adept at hiding his surprise that his wife's usual partner on cases wanted to speak to him instead of her.

"Rand?"

"Hi, Ian. I just need to ask you about something you were working on a while back."

"Well, sure." Ian still sounded puzzled, but willing enough to help.

"Didn't you say something once about one of your polymers being adapted for use in artificial joints?"

"Yes," Ian said, now in what Rand had come to call his inventor's voice. It was the only time, other than when he spoke of Sam, that his voice held such passion. "It's in the final stages of FDA approval."

"What joints?"

"Hips and knees. It'll last years longer than the best thing out there now. Plus it stays malleable long enough for a very easy insertion. It sets up in the body afterward, making the surgery shorter and less traumatic. People will be up and around in hours."

"Any ETA on the approval?"

"Within six months, we hope."

"Anybody up here going to be qualified with it?"

"You're near Seattle?"

"Yes."

And no, Rand added silently, thinking with a grin of how different this rural area was from the city on the other side of Puget Sound. Many people here said "other side" as if the words were capitalized, indicating another world.

"I think so. I think some people at the University of Washington are already involved. I could check."

"Do that, would you?"

"Sure. Anything else?"

"That'll do it. Thanks Ian."

"Any time. Here's Sam again."

"What's up with that?" she asked when she came back on the phone.

"Just somebody up here that might benefit from your husband's genius."

"He is that," Sam said. She sounded happier than he'd ever heard since he'd known her. It made no sense that one of Redstone's best security agents and a man who was sometimes called the absentminded professor would fit so well, but they did.

"Getting personally involved?" she asked. Obviously she meant the inquiry about Ian's project, but the first thing that popped into his head was Kate.

"No," he said quickly. Apparently too quickly, because he knew the instant she spoke that he'd triggered Sam's finely tuned radar.

"Rand Singleton! You know better than to get personally involved," she admonished.

To quash the tempting images her words conjured up,

Rand decided to go ahead and make the obvious point. "Are you the pot, or the kettle?"

"Exactly my point," Sam said. "Look what happened to me."

The next sounds he heard were a thump and an exaggerated yelp from Sam; obviously Ian had thrown something at her. After that Sam laughed and hung up so quickly Rand had little doubt what was about to happen in the Gamble household. With a sigh he disconnected. He didn't begrudge his partner—and friend—her newfound happiness, she'd certainly paid her dues and then some, but sometimes he felt oddly lonely, like a kid whose best friend suddenly didn't have time for him anymore.

And that thought made him feel as if he were being childish, so he told himself to get over it. It wasn't as if he was really foolish enough to get involved with someone when he was on a case, let alone a prime suspect in that case. Of course, Sam had known better too, and now look at her.

Yeah, she's deliriously happy, he thought glumly.

"And nobody deserves it more than her," he told himself aloud and rather sternly. Besides, she'd been guarding Ian—he hadn't been a suspect.

He stuck his cell phone in the charger and trotted downstairs. Dorothy had promised a meat loaf he would never forget tonight, and he could already smell it up here. When he got to the kitchen, he stopped in his tracks; Kate was setting the dining room table. When he ate with the Crawfords they usually sat at the small kitchen table that was set up for two but could squeeze three. So obviously Kate was staying for dinner.

He found himself smiling before he realized it was happening. When he caught himself, he assured himself that it was simply that the more time he spent with her the more chance he had at determining what, if anything, she had to do with the thefts. It would help his investigation if he could presume on their newly made peace and get closer to her. In a strictly business sense, of course. If he could think about business at all with her walking around in those jeans and that floaty, gauzy-looking yellow top that made her eyes glow golden and was already driving him crazy the way it blew over her body.

The meat loaf was as promised, hearty fare with a bit of a kick. Rand had just made a mental note to ask Dorothy what was in it, for his mother, when the teasing started. Walt had been talking about removing the tree out back, a big maple that was dying, when Dorothy started to chuckle.

"Don't start, Gram!" Kate ordered, gesturing with her fork.

"Oh, please, it's one of my favorite memories."

Kate groaned, and Walt looked at his wife. "You say that now," he pointed out, "but at the time you were beside yourself."

"Well it was a brand-new dress," Dorothy said.

"It was stiff and scratchy and horridly uncomfortable," Kate said flatly.

"Not for long," Dorothy said ruefully.

"That's what you get," Walt said, "for trying to make a tomboy a girly-girl."

"I wasn't a tomboy," Kate protested.

"You weren't a girly-girl, either," her grandfather pointed his own fork at her.

"You were," Dorothy intoned somewhat regally, "a delightful combination of both, as the situation suited."

"Well, except for that time with the tree," Kate said, and

Rand saw the corners of her mouth twitch. She was fighting a laugh, he could see it, and he loved the sparkle it put in her eyes.

Although he inwardly recoiled from his own thoughts, he didn't think anything had shown in his face. That is, until Walt pointed out, "It's rude to discuss this in front of Rand, without explaining."

Kate gave Rand a sideways look. The sparkle of humor was still there. "There's not much to explain. I was eleven. Gram bought me this awful, stiff, frilly dress. It hurt just to wear."

Rand flicked a glance from her to her grandmother, who was smiling widely, and back again.

"And you took care of this how?"

"I fell out of the maple tree."

He blinked. "What?"

"I'd climbed it to hide, so I didn't have to go to whatever it was, a wedding or something."

"And promptly fell face-down in the big puddle underneath," Dorothy said, her smile a grin now.

Kate's grin broke loose now. "I was mud from head to toe."

"I bet the dress was softer then," Rand said.

Kate laughed then. It was a lovely, silvery sound, just as it had been the other day, and he felt a sudden, fervent hope that he wouldn't have to do anything that would quell that laugh.

"It was," Kate agreed. "Problem solved, as far as I could see. Softer dress, didn't have to go to the wedding, I was happy."

"So, are you still a problem solver?"

"That she is," Walt said proudly, but Rand noticed Kate went suddenly still. She lowered her eyes to her plate as if to avoid her grandfather's eyes.

"Everybody says she's lucky to work for Redstone," Dorothy put in, "but I think they're lucky to have her."

"From everything I've heard," Rand said neutrally, "it's usually mutual with Redstone."

Kate's gaze shot to his face. "From everything you've heard?"

"It's hard to avoid hearing about it when Josh Redstone's face is on the cover of *Time, Newsweek* or *Forbes* about every other week," Walt said, nothing but respect in his voice. "That man's a marvel, all right."

You don't know the half of it, Rand thought. "Have you ever met him?" he said, careful to make his tone casual, idle.

"He interviewed me," Kate said.

"Oh?"

His surprise wasn't that Josh had interviewed an applicant for what was a fairly low-ranking position, at least relative to the size of Redstone itself. He often did that. His surprise was that it hadn't been in her file. Josh rarely made mistakes about people, and if he had personally hired someone, that would be a factor he hadn't taken into account. A factor definitely in her favor.

Which was, he realized suddenly, likely why it wasn't in the file he'd seen. Draven wouldn't want him going in biased, and knowing this woman had made it past Josh's radar would definitely have done that.

Of course, she likely was clean, back then. Perhaps it was only now that she'd become desperate—desperate to help the people she'd made clear meant more to her than anything on earth. People did some things they would never ordinarily do when the people they loved were in need. There was no doubt she loved her grandparents enough to do whatever it took to take care of them.

But the thought that she might have crossed the line so

far as to steal from Redstone made him faintly ill, and it was all he could do to finish Dorothy's tasty meat loaf.

Kate couldn't remember the last time she'd felt well-rested. They were coming up on another shipment of the pumps, and her worry was beginning to build. That resulted in less sleep, which seemed to compound itself; the less she got, the less she got.

She shook her head and groaned inwardly; even her ramblings didn't make sense anymore. She unlocked her center desk drawer and pulled out the copies of the two police reports on the previous thefts. She practically knew them by heart, but still she took them out every other day or so for another read, hoping to see something she'd missed before, or something that hadn't meant anything before but did now. She never did, but that didn't stop her from trying.

It was impossible. She shoved the reports back in the drawer and slammed it shut. Nothing ever changed. The trucks were loaded and secured by the night shift. The only one who ever came near it after that was the night mechanic doing a routine maintenance check on the vehicle, which never involved him entering the cargo area. The drivers arrived early in the morning, picked up the vehicle, doors still locked. When they arrived at the buyer's facility, they were still locked. There was no sign of any tampering. Yet the precious cargo was missing, leaving nothing but empty boxes.

It gnawed at her, and she felt it was her fault, no matter what anyone said. And she was going to feel that way until the thefts were resolved and the guilty party caught. It wasn't her reputation she was worried about, at least not solely. The thefts had to stop, if for no other reason than people really needed those pumps. It was the sensor that made it miraculous—the sensor that continually tested the patient's blood and dispensed necessary insulin before any damage could be done.

Eventually Redstone hoped that the pumps would control some of the worst side effects of diabetes, like blindness and amputations. She'd heard they were also looking into the possibility the sensor could be adapted for other needed substances, such as human growth hormone. And that somebody would steal something with the potential to help so many people made her faintly ill.

She was still pondering it a few minutes later when she came out of the market. She'd stopped there to get a few things to restock her cupboards after eating at her grandparents for the past three days. It was only because Gram kept fixing her favorite meals, she told herself. It had nothing to do with the fact that Rand had also been joining them.

She yanked her mind back to where it needed to be. She just didn't see how the thefts could be happening. She'd talked to everyone who ever had access to those trucks or the shipments, and she couldn't believe any of them were involved. She couldn't think of anyone who would be tempted to steal something, that they all worked so hard to produce and get out there to people.

Finding a discontented worker at Redstone wasn't easy. She supposed they were there, but she certainly hadn't come across any of them. In fact, she guessed most of the people here would be as outraged by the thefts as she was, hating the idea of anything jeopardizing their jobs with the company they'd quickly come to love.

And the drivers were Redstone people too, so there was no way they'd be lying about being involved, and they were always there, watching, until the recipient signed the papers that the full shipment had been received.

So how was it happening? What was she missing? There had to be something she wasn't—

She blinked as sunlight glinted on an unnatural hair color in the distance. Mel. With a small bag in her hand, the girl was crossing the parking lot from the drugstore. Kate considered calling out to her, but it was the girl's day off and she might not be glad to be reminded she'd have to be back to work tomorrow.

Kate returned to her thoughts as she walked toward her car, shifting her own bag of groceries to her hip as she switched her keys to her right hand. Instinctively she looked up again for Mel.

The girl was looking right at her. And her expression was unmistakable. She looked startled. And…caught. Mel's head jerked sideways as she broke the eye contact abruptly. Kate watched as the girl got hastily into her old blue sedan, started the engine and exited the parking lot with a squeal of tires on pavement.

She couldn't have made it more clear she was dodging Kate if she'd shouted it.

And Kate's heart plummeted to her shoes.

Chapter 9

Rand yawned, then stretched. It had been a long week. He'd been on watch every day, and some nights until dawn streaked the sky. He wasn't even sure what he was looking for, only that he hadn't seen it. He had photos of everyone who came and went from Redstone, though, and had a good idea of the normal activity pattern.

And an even better idea of Kate's activity pattern.

She hadn't varied it much. Only occasionally did she leave the building during the day. Twice, including today, she'd left to pick up lunch for half the staff, judging by the bags she'd returned with.

Speaking of food, he thought, he was going to knock off early tonight. His last communication from Redstone had said there was a shipment of the insulin pumps going out day after tomorrow, so he was going to need sleep to stake that out. Besides, Dorothy had said something about chicken and dumplings tonight, and he didn't want to miss that.

He hadn't thought so much about what was for dinner in years, and if he didn't watch it, he was going to end up going home ten pounds heavier than when he arrived, he told himself.

That he didn't want to think about going home just yet was not something that concerned him. He was, after all, in the middle of a case, so going home was naturally far from his mind. Naturally.

He no sooner walked in the Crawford's front door—sniffing appreciatively at the aroma that filled the house—than he heard Dorothy's voice.

"You're in trouble, young man!"

The spry, gray-haired woman was actually waving a wooden spoon at him, her expression stern. Behind her, in the kitchen, he saw Kate, looking amused but also puzzled.

"Just what do you think you're doing?" Dorothy continued in a voice that matched her expression.

Rand held up his hands, palms out, in self-defense. "You're going to have to tell me, since I have no idea."

"Don't play dumb with me, Rand Singleton. If you think I can't read Elwood Turner like a book, you're mistaken."

"Oh." The grocery store. Now he knew.

"Yes, oh."

"I rented a room," he said firmly. "That didn't include you feeding me practically every night and morning, and packing me lunches on top of it."

"One extra mouth doesn't add that much," Dorothy said, but the spoon at least had stopped waving.

"It does when it's mine," Rand pointed out, somewhat ruefully. "I eat as much as both of you put together, and you know it."

Dorothy smiled then. "It does my heart good to see a boy eat hearty."

"And it does my heart good to know I'm paying my way," Rand retorted.

"What on earth are you two squabbling about?" Kate was wiping her hands on a dish towel as she came toward them.

"The fact that Elwood wouldn't let me pay for my weekly groceries today. Said they'd already been paid for. For next week, too."

Kate gave him a sideways look, her expression a mixture of surprise that irked him, and pleasure that warmed him.

"I'd be spending more than that if I was eating out all the time," he pointed out. "Besides," he grinned at Dorothy, "it wouldn't be nearly as good."

"Oh, you," she said, but her cheeks colored prettily.

"Am I forgiven?" From the smile and hug she gave him he guessed he was. On that front, anyway.

"That was very nice," Kate said after her grandmother retreated to the kitchen to finish her preparations.

"It's only fair. I've ended up eating here a lot, although it was never my intention."

"She loves to cook," Kate said.

"And does it well," Rand said, with a wry smile and a pat to his stomach. "I'm going to take more than memories of this place home with me."

Kate smiled. The same sweet, generous smile he'd just seen on her grandmother's face. He doubted his luck would run to getting the hug, too.

What the hell are you thinking?

He answered himself. *Like a guy who hasn't had a hug from a woman he finds attractive in far too long.*

There. At least he was being honest, admitting he was attracted to her. Maybe that was the best way, instead of trying to dodge it, just confront it head-on and get past it. Maybe if Sam hadn't tried so long to deny what she was feeling for Ian, she wouldn't have gotten in so deep that by the time she quit denying it, it was too late.

Of course, then she wouldn't be married to Ian, nor be so deliriously happy it made him smile just to see her. And he was totally convinced they were forever, despite the warnings they'd all heard countless times about getting involved on a job. And Ian had had to get over Sam's subterfuge of posing as his neighbor to hide his real purpose.

And aren't you doing the same thing to Kate?

The thought, unwelcome on so many levels, made him grimace inwardly. He smothered a sigh as he gathered up plates and silverware to set the table, as he'd gotten in the habit of doing. Life was too confusing sometimes. He loved his work, wouldn't want to do anything else, but sometimes it complicated what was already complicated enough.

Of course, if it turned out she was guilty, that would end a whole lot of complications.

And cause a whole new batch.

"Someday we'd like to remodel," her grandmother said. "Make the bedroom we're in now a little bigger, and add a bath."

"More like what you had upstairs?" Rand asked as he got up and helped clear the table, as if it was something he did every day. As perhaps he did, Kate thought. He was here more than she was, after all.

Her grandmother nodded, and again Kate tried to quash the pang of guilt and pain the casual discussion was causing her. She should be taking better care of them, like they had her. But every cent she made was earmarked for bills and necessities for all of them, and she had little left for things that were anything less than crucial.

Her grandfather didn't look too comfortable with the discussion either, and Kate knew it was because he felt responsible; it was his bum knees that had forced them to move downstairs.

"What if you made the bedroom the bath, and turned the garage into the bedroom?" Rand said as he neatly put the dishes in the dishwasher. *A housebroken man, how about that,* Kate thought. "They connect right there, don't they?"

"I thought about that," Gramps said from the table. "I think it would work."

"Sure it would. Or, you could steal the laundry room for the bathroom, and kick out the back wall to enlarge the bedroom," Rand said, apparently running with a ton of ideas now.

"Then we wouldn't have to build a new garage," her grandfather said.

"It would be expensive either way, though," her grandmother said.

"We'll find a way, Gram," Kate said. She had no idea how, but she would. Somehow.

"What about something else in the meantime?" Rand asked. "Something like one of those stairway power lifts?"

"Those aren't cheap, either," Gramps said.

"And I have to say, I don't mind not going up stairs all the time myself," Gram said, reaching out to pat the hand of her husband of over fifty years.

"Okay, then start planning," Rand suggested. "That way, when the time comes, you'll be ready to go. Besides, it's fun to dream, even if it never happens."

"I suppose we could do that," Gram said.

Kate kept quiet, torn. She wasn't sure this was a good thing. She didn't want them to get their hearts set on a plan and then not be able to do it for a long time. Until she was able to dig out from under, anyway.

"My sister's studying to be a designer," Rand said. "I'm sure she could rough something out for you, if you gave her the basics of what you want. I can help you measure, and brainstorm the plan. Then you could at least get an estimate."

"Really?" Gram perked up at that.

"Sure. Then you'll know what you're dealing with. You may decide it's more trouble than it's worth."

"Oh, my," Gram said, excitement in her voice. "Now I want to go get some of my magazines to look at."

She hastily put the last of the dishes into the washer, pulled off her apron and headed off to the den.

"Now look what you've started, boy," Gramps said, but he was chuckling when he said it.

"Are you kidding?" Rand said. "It'll take her a year to decide exactly what she wants. I bought you breathing room."

Gramps burst out laughing. It was a sound she hadn't heard from him in a long while, and it made her smile. And she directed the smile at the man who had made it happen. He smiled back, warm and beautiful. Her heart seemed to falter, then jumped to catch up.

Uh-oh.

She turned to finish wiping off the dining table, staring down at the dark oak finish, wondering just how much trouble she was already in, and how she was going to keep from getting into more.

"Damn."

Rand said it under his breath, aware of the disappointment, anger and regret behind the curse.

Kate was involved. He wasn't sure just how, yet, but he knew better than to believe it was coincidence that on the night before a shipment of the pumps, she had slipped out of her house at eleven o'clock. She'd never left her house after she'd been in for the night, not since he'd been here. He'd wondered at it, wondered why the woman seemed to have no social life outside her grandparents. Were there just no single men in Summer Harbor, or were they all blind? If he'd been here, he would have been after her like— He broke off his own thought as an unexpected rush of heat flooded him.

With an effort he dragged his attention back to the job at hand. He shifted in the driver's seat of the rental. He waited as Kate walked to the garage that sat apart from the little cottage-style house she lived in. A few moments later her car emerged and headed down the driveway. At the street, where he was parked, she turned left, heading toward the highway.

And Redstone?

He stifled a sigh as he followed her. He hadn't wanted to believe it. Knowing about the shipment, he'd staked out her house, praying it would be for nothing. How much he had hoped, he didn't realize until that hope was shattered.

He was feeling so grim about Kate's actions that it worried him. Worried him because he didn't like what it said about how far he was down a path he'd sworn he would never travel. He was so deep in pondering his own uncharacteristic actions that when she turned right instead of left on the highway, he was caught off guard.

She wasn't headed for Redstone.

He told himself the thing that spiked through him then was curiosity, not a rekindling of hope. It was a challenge to follow her. It was so dark out here, in this place of no streetlights and towering trees that blocked even what moonlight there was. Still, it wasn't so bad here on the highway, where whatever traffic was on the roads at this time of night seemed to be. But if she turned onto one of the smaller side streets or narrow gravel driveways, it was going to be tricky to follow her without her realizing it.

When she did turn right again, he hung back as far as he thought he could without risking losing her altogether. The road she turned on was paved and had two full lanes, so he guessed it was well traveled enough to have two cars on it even this late without rousing suspicion.

But then she turned down a narrow, one-lane road, and he knew he had to be careful. He slowed and flipped off his headlights, and stopped just enough into the intersection to watch her taillights. He saw her car proceed about a quarter mile down the narrow road and then pull to the right and stop, in the black shadow of a big evergreen.

The street was so narrow, and so quiet, he knew a second car would draw attention. He didn't dare get too close. Finally he settled on parking in a wide area at the end of the street, far enough back that she couldn't see him, and not in front of any of the houses where residents might be stirred to curiosity.

He dug into his utility bag and brought out a pair of night vision binoculars. He turned them on and raised them to his eyes. And immediately lowered them again when the familiar green glow failed to appear. He checked the switch to make sure it was on. It was. He turned it off, then back on. Still nothing.

Rand swore under his breath. He didn't have time to try to figure out what was wrong now. Not that he could have; he could operate the things with the best of them, but repairing them wasn't in his repertoire. He'd send for another pair, but for now he was going to have to wing it.

He waited. And watched. And waited.

Because of the dark shadow of that tree, he couldn't see what, if anything, she was doing. But he could see that she wasn't getting out of her car. He tried to fix their geographic position in his head. She had turned right each time.

Three times.

Which put them right back in the vicinity of Redstone, albeit, judging by the distance they'd traveled, the back side. Which was perhaps the perfect place. There were no tall, razor wire fences around Redstone. Any Redstone. That wasn't Josh's style. Here a simple wood fence that blended with the landscape was the only demarcation between Redstone and the open land beyond. It wouldn't be hard to get over it. If it were him, he'd simply remove a panel and refasten it loosely, so that it looked solid but could be taken out in seconds.

He'd talked to Josh about it, on another case at another Redstone facility. The multibillionaire had acknowledged that it wasn't the best security, but added in his quiet drawl, "That's why I've got the best security team in the world. I won't live in a fortress, Rand, and I don't want my people to have to work in one."

And yet Josh was quite capable of adopting a fortress mentality when motivated. Let something happen to or threaten one of his own, and he could circle the wagons and fight back with the best of them. And it didn't have to be one of the higher-ups at Redstone to garner this kind of protection, either. He'd sent out the troops just as strongly for inventor Ian Gamble as he had for point man Noah Rider. In Josh's view, if you worked for Redstone, you were his responsibility. And he took care of his own.

He leaned forward slightly, peering through the darkness at Kate's vehicle. All he could see was a shadow he knew was her sitting inside the car, not moving, her head turned slightly to the left as if she were watching as intently as he was.

Maybe she was, he thought with a grimace. Maybe this was the escape route for the thieves and she was playing lookout. With a repeat of his lecture to himself not to get emotionally involved, he settled in to watch with a critical eye. If necessary, he would come back tomorrow in daylight to find out exactly what could be seen from where she was. He would walk the street and see where it was in relation to Redstone—and if there was a back way to get from one to the other.

Time passed. A car did leave from the end of the block, and while Kate watched, she didn't follow. So neither did Rand. He opened and sipped at the caffeinated soda he'd brought with him. Next would be the cookies left over from the lunch Dorothy had packed for him. He felt a twinge of guilt at eating her baking while spying on her granddaughter, but if Kate were guilty, that would be the least of his sins before this was over.

At nearly five in the morning her taillights came on again and he jerked straight upright. She drove down to the end of the street where it appeared to dead-end, turned and headed back toward the cross street. And him. He glanced quickly, saw that his car was covered with dew, and would likely look like a local car that had been parked here all night. It shouldn't even draw her attention. And even if it did, in the dark, where colors weren't clear, she'd have no way of knowing it was his rental. There were many of this model on the streets, even in tiny Summer Harbor.

He ducked down as she came up to the corner. He could hear her car clearly, and knew from the sound she'd turned back the way she'd come. He waited until she was far enough away before sitting up again and adjusting his mirror to watch her retrace her earlier route.

He started the engine, quickly whipped a U-turn and sped after her. And in a few moments he was watching from across the street as she pulled back into her own driveway and into the garage. The big door descended. He saw her shadowy figure as she came out through the small side garage door and walked back to the house.

She went in quickly, so quickly he wondered with some irritation whether she'd even locked the front door. A light came on inside, then went out. Another light toward the back of the house did the same.

Darkness settled down once again.

And Rand was left knowing little more than he had before.

Chapter 10

"Damn!"

The oath burst from Kate's lips before she could stop it. They'd been hit again. She nearly slammed down the phone receiver, the only thing stopping her being the fact that it wasn't the fault of the poor messenger. Jim Saltzman, the driver of the delivery truck, was already upset enough. This was the second time for him, and he knew perfectly well that the most likely time for the thefts to occur was while the shipment was in his custody.

But he swore on his children's lives he didn't know anything about them, and Kate believed him. Jim had been with Redstone a long time, had in fact transferred here after working fifteen years at Redstone Technologies in Los Angeles. He practically worshipped Josh Redstone, and Kate simply couldn't picture him ever doing anything against the man or the company. Maybe she was naive, but she had him near the bottom of her possible suspect list, despite his having the best opportunity to pull off the crimes.

She yawned widely as she sat up in bed. She'd been trying to catch at least a little sleep when Jim's distressed call had awakened her. She felt exhausted. How much of it was purely physical she didn't know; she'd been tired ever since the first theft had occurred.

As she got up and quickly showered and dressed, she felt as if she'd been beaten. Gramps often used the phrase "dragged through a knothole, backwards" to describe how he felt after a hard day. She'd always thought it merely a quaint, colorful old saying. Now she knew exactly what it meant.

She felt a hollowness inside as she drove to work. She loved working at Redstone, but if she didn't get this problem solved—and stopped—she doubted she'd have her job much longer. Joshua Redstone might be the greatest guy in the world to work for, as most of his people said, but even he wasn't going to take this for long.

The hollow feeling grew as she entered the building and caught people watching her go by, much as they watched a funeral procession, the gratefulness that they weren't in her position clear on their faces. She plastered a smile on her face, as if nothing was wrong. Someone on the inside was involved in this, and she'd be darned if she'd let them see her in a panic. But when she got into her office, she closed the door behind her.

She paced from the door to her desk and back again, as she had so often in the past two months, her mind darting desperately into any corner where a solution might be hiding. She and security guard Brian Fisher had spent hours trying to brainstorm answers. At this point, the only answer she could come up with was to drive the darn truck herself, and she wasn't sure she wouldn't do it at this rate.

Gradually her pace slowed. There was nothing she could do about the thefts at this moment, so she might as well start the day's work. There was certainly enough of it. The pumps weren't the only thing that were made and shipped out of Redstone Northwest, and she had a lot of other responsibilities.

At least, she did for now.

Maybe I should just resign, she thought. *Save Mr. Redstone the trouble of firing me.*

It was then she knew how tired she was. She'd never been a quitter. And while she hated the idea of hanging around to be fired, she hated more the idea of giving up on a problem that was hers to solve.

And to her surprise, she found she hated the idea of letting down the quiet, gray-eyed man who'd hired her. She hadn't seen him in person since that day two years ago, but he was as fresh in her mind as if it had been yesterday. She'd sensed the muted pain about him, and she would do a great deal to avoid adding to it.

The storm descended upon her quickly then. Another police report, with all the questions she couldn't answer. A call from the detective assigned to the case, who made it clear she thought Redstone had an internal problem—and given the circumstances, Kate couldn't really disagree. A visit from the plant manager, who in typical Redstone fashion was more worried than angry, although she doubted it would take much more to push him over that line.

When her office was finally cleared, she wondered how long it would be before she herself was pushed over that line. She'd gone through a stage of shock and disbelief, which had turned to hurt when she realized the perpetrator was likely on the inside. Now an edge of panic was creeping in as she felt more and more helpless to do anything.

She tried lecturing herself; she was competent, efficient

and smart. She'd handled a high-level job at a frenetic investment company for years. She could handle this.

Her pep talk sounded good, she even believed it. Except for that last part. How was she going to handle this when she couldn't even figure out how the crimes were being committed?

"Have dinner with me."

Kate looked at him so blankly he had to assume she either found the suggestion ridiculous, or had completely forgotten he was in the room. Neither possibility was particularly flattering. Or in the least encouraging. Quickly he rethought his approach.

"I thought I'd take your grandparents out," he said quickly, nodding toward the kitchen of her grandparents house, where her grandmother was audibly pondering tonight's dinner. "Dorothy's been cooking for me for days now, it seems the least I can do."

He had thought the inclusion of her grandparents would make it easier for her, but it didn't seem to. She was now looking at him with what appeared to be suspicion.

And then, even as he watched, she gave a sigh and the expression faded. *As if she'd consciously fought it down,* he thought. And he'd learned to go with those gut reactions. All the Redstone security team had received extensive training in the psychological aspects of their work, body language and other telltale signs. As Draven always said, if you can't read your quarry, you could soon find *yourself* the quarry. Rand didn't like applying that maxim to Kate, but there it was.

"They'll want you to go," he said. "In fact, if you don't, they probably won't."

A flicker of a grimace flashed across her face, but vanished so quickly he couldn't be sure what it was in reaction to.

"All right," she finally said, but her tone told him her assent was only because he was likely right about her grandparents refusing the rare night out if she didn't accompany them.

So, he thought, despite her apology, suspicion was still her first reaction to him. Apparently this time he'd come up against somebody who didn't buy into the baby-faced innocence that he had so often used to his advantage. Obviously he was going to have to work harder at gaining her trust.

It wasn't like he hadn't had to earn trust before. Not everyone trusted him on sight. But people did more often than not, he admitted ruefully, only now realizing how much he had grown to depend on that to get his job done.

As he was up in his rented room getting ready, he pondered how to go about earning this particular woman's trust. If she still truly suspected he was up to something that would somehow hurt her grandparents, then he wasn't sure how to change her mind. Time might do it, but that was a commodity he didn't have in great supply.

He pulled on a sweater and straightened it, still thinking. And not liking what he was coming up with.

He could leave. Simply say his work was done, he'd gotten his photos, and move out, leaving Dorothy and Walt unscathed, proving he'd not been after anything at all from them. Of course, if he did that, whether she trusted him or not was a moot point. Not to mention that it would make completing the investigation much more difficult—especially if he was seen after supposedly leaving. And if he was spotted in this town, he was certain that his presence would be reported directly to one of the Crawfords. It seemed to be the way things worked around here.

If she didn't trust him because she was involved in the thefts, then nothing he could do would change that. And in the end he'd be the one responsible for bringing her down. He didn't like the feel of that at all. But it was his job, and he wouldn't be the first Redstone security agent who'd had to do something he didn't relish. Redstone was truly like a huge family, and when the rare black sheep sneaked through, no one was happy about it.

The fact that he couldn't easily dismiss Kate's possible involvement set off warning bells in his head, but he didn't know what to do about it.

He could call for help, he thought as he ran a comb through his hair, a useless exercise since he knew it would flop forward again the moment he took a single step. It always had, and he'd resigned himself to the probability it always would; the men in his family had a history of keeping their hair into their eighties.

Yes, he could call for help, have somebody else on the team step in. It would be awkward to explain, and delay the investigation.

But they wouldn't care about who was involved, only solving the case.

The realization hit him suddenly and hard. A new investigator would see Kate only as a suspect, and the most likely one at that. Might zero in on her and see guilt in her edginess and some of her actions, and wouldn't know her well enough to cast doubt on those suspicions.

And do you?

"Shut up," he muttered under his breath to the voice in his head that picked the worst times to speak and worse things to say. He *did* know she was kind, generous and very, very smart.

And sexy. Don't forget that, he added to himself wryly.

As he left his rented haven and went down the stairs, he discarded his idea of calling in someone else. He was in this investigation, it was his job to handle, and handle it he would.

He just had to figure out how to handle Kate Crawford, and that decision wasn't coming as easily.

Kate couldn't remember the last time she'd heard her grandparents laugh so much. She hadn't completely realized how solemn they'd become until tonight. It made her feel guilty for not noticing before this, and grateful to hear their laughter now. And, she had to admit, grateful to Rand, since he was the one who had managed it. His stories of his travels around the world, especially the one about the cab driver in Madrid, were a wonderful diversion.

"It's good to hear you laugh, honey," her grandmother said, startling Kate with the similarity to her own thoughts.

"You don't laugh enough," her grandfather intoned with a nod.

She had been laughing too, she realized then. She'd been so focused on her grandparents' elevated mood that she hadn't thought about herself. And her grandparents were right, it had been a long time since she had laughed. Since the day of the first theft, she thought. Yet he'd managed to distract her from that, and from this latest theft.

"She has a wonderful laugh," Rand said softly. He was, thankfully, looking at her grandparents, so he didn't see the color that rose in her cheeks.

She looked at Rand with a new appreciation. He was even more charming than she'd thought. And, she admitted ruefully, even better-looking. In the casual wear she'd seen him in up until tonight he was handsome enough, but in the sweater he'd donned, a heavy pullover in a deep blue that made his eyes fairly glow, he was…spectacular, she thought wryly.

And young, she reminded herself. Too young. She tore her gaze from him in the moment before he turned in her direction. She studied her dessert plate. Suddenly the landslide of chocolate on it wasn't so appealing. She set down her fork, wondering who had selected that sweater for him. Female, no doubt. A woman would realize what that color would do for his eyes. Not to mention the high unlikelihood of a man like Rand not having a woman in his life. Perhaps more than one. As many, she told herself, as he wanted to have. You didn't look like he did and not have them beating down your door.

All of which was, she told herself rather sternly, academic. It wasn't as if she had any interest in him that way, of course. But she could appreciate. From a distance, anyway. As her grandmother had often teased her, "It doesn't cost a thing to window shop."

But any further idiotic musings on her part could end up costing her in one way or another. And she didn't have much emotional serenity to spare. Her ex had begun the process of decimation the death of her child had finished. She'd fought back, but there were moments when it was still touch and go. So it would stop. Now.

Decision made, Kate determined to treat him like any other casual acquaintance. In line with that, she offered to split the bill with him; he'd chosen the best and most expensive restaurant for thirty miles around. He thanked her, but refused the offer.

"It was my suggestion, my treat. And my pleasure," he added with a smile that almost made her forget all the vows she'd just made to herself.

"Thank you, then," she said, turning to open the door for her grandparents as Rand paid the bill.

The bite of approaching winter was in the air, and Kate drew in a deep breath, savoring the clean, crisp feel of it. She loved this time of year, and took pleasure in the simple act of watching her breath in the cold.

"You really love this place, don't you?"

Rand had slowed to her strolling pace, letting her grandparents move ahead. She nodded. "I do. It's home. Always has been, no matter where I've gone. I only left because I got a job offer I thought I couldn't refuse." She gave him a sideways glance. "What's home for you?"

He gave a one-shouldered shrug. "Southern California, I suppose. That's where I grew up, anyway. But for me, home's wherever my folks are."

Kate felt a sudden tightness in her throat. She wondered what it must be like, to have parents like that. To have parents who were the core of your life, always there for you, and you for them. She had that kind of relationship with her grandparents, but it wasn't the same. Their relationship came with the built-in knowledge that she'd lose them too soon, too early. She tried not to think about it, but she had learned long ago painful thoughts didn't go away just because she wanted them to.

"Your mom and dad must be wonderful." She heard the wistfulness in her voice too late to stop it. "Don't get me wrong," she said hastily. "Gram and Gramps have been wonderful, and I love them very dearly. But I always wondered what it would have been like if my parents had been…different."

He looked at her for a long moment before saying quietly, "You make me want to call mine and thank them."

"Do that," she said, rather fervently.

"I do, frequently. But maybe an extra thank-you won't hurt."

He's nice, Kate thought later as they climbed into his rented SUV. She had to work to remember how suspicious she'd been of him at first. But after tonight she just couldn't doubt any longer that he was as nice as he seemed.

He drove smoothly, taking what seemed to her extra care she assumed was for her grandparents, which she appreciated. And when they pulled up at the house, he quickly got out and came around to help them out of the car and walk them up to the door. She followed, but said good-night at the door, not wanting Gram to make the inevitable offer of coffee or tea; it was late for them, and she knew they were tired.

"I'll be in after I walk Kate to her car," Rand told them and closed the door.

"I'm fine," she began.

"Of course," he agreed, but stayed beside her.

"You don't need to do this, I'm parked right here."

"I know."

She wasn't sure what to say to that, so said nothing. She got out her keys and opened the driver's door. He held it for her as she got in.

"Thank you for going tonight," he said.

"Thank you. They don't get out often enough."

"How about tomorrow?"

She blinked. "Tomorrow?"

"Dinner. I want to try this steak place I found over near the ferry landing."

"Sloan's?"

"Yeah, I think that's it."

"It's a good restaurant."

"Excellent," he said. "I'll pick you up at your place at seven."

Before she could even respond he closed her car door, stepped back, and waved. She reached down to open her window, but he'd already turned on his heel and headed for the house at a trot, leaving her gaping after him. And wondering exactly when she'd agreed to go on a date with him.

Chapter 11

Rand struggled to stay focused. He'd been running short on sleep for days now. For all the good his constant watching had done; the facility had been hit again. And he still had no idea how it was being done.

Nor could he, no matter how much he might want to, eliminate Kate from the suspect list. He didn't know what she'd been up to on the night of the last theft, but the fact that she had varied her routine on that night in particular sent up a red flag he couldn't afford to ignore.

But at least he felt like he was making progress on that front. He wasn't used to having to work so hard to get closer to a woman. And the moment that thought formed in his head he grimaced at the arrogance of it, even though it was true and had been most of his life. He'd tried never to abuse it—his mother had seen to that—and he didn't think he had. The knowledge that his looks were all many people saw was in the past. Why he'd fallen *so* hard for Donna, who had seen him at his worst.

He pushed the memories away and turned back to the present situation.

But while Kate might not be eager to spend time with him, she no longer dodged him, and she'd actually let him get away with the steamroller routine about dinner tonight.

Of course, if he was going to be at all coherent on that occasion, he thought, he was going to have to get some sleep. Normally he could run at length on four or five hours a night, but he hadn't been getting even that lately. Mostly because when he did get to bed he wasn't sleeping. Not well, anyway. He spent too much time thinking about the thefts.

And Kate.

And coming up with few answers about either of them.

He was pleased when he arrived at her door to find her ready to go; he'd been half convinced she would back out. She was dressed simply, in a white, silky-looking blouse and tailored black slacks, but he'd been in the casual Northwest long enough now to realize that this was fancy dress. Her hair was loose, minus her usual clip, and the shifting gleam of it as she walked made his breath catch. Her eyes seemed more golden than ever and he wondered if she'd used some subtle makeup. Then he wondered if she'd done it for him, or the restaurant they were headed to. Then told himself not to be an idiot, the woman had shown no sign of wanting to flatter him.

Still, he complimented her as smoothly as he could.

"Thank you," she said, and left it at that. No dissembling, no self-deprecation, just a simple acceptance. Either she was used to compliments—or she thought he was just being polite. He had no idea which was more likely.

"You look nice yourself," she said, surprising him.

"I— Thank you," he said in turn, following her lead. And realizing with no small amount of ruefulness that in his case, he was certain she was just being polite. He was struck, not for the first time, with a strange wish that this date was for real, that they really were just two people getting to know each other out of a mutual interest.

Shaking it off, at least for the moment, he tried to focus on the job at hand. Until, as they waited for their meal, she startled him again by asking him out of the blue, "Is there a Mrs. Singleton?"

He blinked. And said with full intent, "Yes."

"Oh."

Did she sound disappointed? He couldn't tell. Which irritated him; he was usually better at reading people. But maybe, just maybe, he was making progress. Relieved at that idea, he watched her face carefully as he gave her the explanation.

"I mean my mother, of course. No Mrs. Rand Singletons around."

Her mouth quirked.

"Sorry," he said, grinning. "Couldn't resist."

"Cute."

Her expression told him she accepted the joke, weak as it was. The grin ceased as he continued. "Anyway, I was close once, but it didn't happen."

It was a rather bloodless way of speaking of what had at the time been the biggest emotional disaster of his life, he thought. It had taken him a long time and a lot of effort to reach that sort of calm about it, and even now it caused a twinge.

"I'm sorry."

"It was for the best," he said. And somewhat belatedly

realized the logical next step in a normal conversation. "So, what about you?" he asked, silently chewing himself out for forgetting for a moment that she had no idea how much he already knew about her.

"Married once," she said. "Didn't last."

He knew there was more to it, but he merely nodded. "It happens," he said.

"Yes."

There was an undertone in that one word that spoke volumes. It was subtle, and had he not known about Kate's past, he might have missed it. He wasn't the only one with scars sitting at this table—he just didn't know how deep hers ran.

Over dinner the conversation turned light, became about the inconsequential things that any casual acquaintances might talk about over dinner. And any time he tried to steer into deeper waters she deftly turned him back. He redoubled his efforts, but that only resulted in her adopting a light, teasing tone that warned him she wasn't taking him at all seriously.

"So where shall we go tomorrow night?" he asked in a last-ditch effort as he calculated the tip and signed the check. She only laughed. He finished, then looked up at her. "I said something funny?"

"No," she said, "you're just acting funny."

"I am?" he asked carefully. "Asking out a very attractive woman is funny?"

She shook her head, her smile never wavering. "Tell me, Rand, did you have crushes on your female teachers when you were in school?"

"What?"

"When you were in school, did you—"

"I heard you. What's that supposed to mean?"

"Just wondering."

"Wondering what?"

She shrugged. "How old are you?"

"Thirty-three."

She looked as surprised as most people did when they learned his age, thanks to that baby face of his that was as much curse as blessing. But that didn't stop her from making what was apparently her point.

"Do you know I'm nearly a decade older than you?" she asked.

In fact, he had known it. The detail had been in her Redstone file. But he had completely forgotten about it because she didn't seem any older than he was, and she certainly didn't look it. And also because he had never imagined it would play into this case.

And it never would have mattered, if you hadn't let things get out of control. Personally out of control, he lectured himself silently.

"Is that why you're acting like I'm one of the kids you mentor?" he asked, aware even as he said it that his voice sounded like one of those kids in a snit.

"I'm forty-one, Rand."

"So?" he said, knowing it sounded lame.

Kate smiled, almost sadly. Then she let out a sigh that implied he was being deliberately stubborn about acknowledging a simple truth.

Perhaps he was, he thought. It bothered him that she would let such a minor thing as age get in the way. Bothered him too much; much more than if this were strictly business. But he couldn't seem to help his reaction.

Out of control was definitely the right way to put it, he muttered inwardly. Whether in frustration or irritation he couldn't have said.

* * *

"You," Dorothy Crawford told her granddaughter, "need to get a life."

Kate sighed, thinking she'd been doing an awful lot of sighing lately. Especially since she'd gone out with Rand last week. "So you've said," she replied neutrally. "Often."

She continued unloading bags of groceries into the cupboards without further comment. Again Mr. Turner had refused to take their money, insisting there was more than enough left out of the money "that young man" had given him to cover today's purchases.

That young man, Kate thought, was a nuisance. He simply wouldn't give up on trying to get her to go out with him again. She had thought pointing out the gap in their ages would have stifled his interest, but it seemed to have done the opposite.

If he just didn't look so young, she thought glumly. Maybe she could get past him being only thirty-three if it wasn't for that.

"—forever?"

She made herself tune back in to her grandmother's words. "What, Gram?"

"I asked you if you were going to let the past rule you forever."

It was unusual for Gram to mention the past—Kate's at least—at all, and she went still.

"Gram," she began.

"Don't you deny it," her grandmother said sternly. "You've held everyone but us at arm's length ever since you came back home."

"I haven't," she protested. "I simply don't have any spare time."

"You make sure you don't have time for anything but work," her grandmother retorted.

"Gram," she tried again.

"You know I don't stick my nose into your business, but I've just got to say that Dan isn't worth this. He's the one who left, the one who couldn't accept. He's the one who didn't have the staying power."

"It has nothing to do with Dan," Kate said, her voice tight.

"Then why are you avoiding going out with Rand?"

"I went to dinner with him," she pointed out.

"Once. And I know he's asked you again."

"Oh? And just how do you know that?"

"He told me."

Great, Kate thought wryly. *Now he's enlisting my own grandmother.*

"He's eight years younger than I am."

"So?"

Her grandmother's echoing of Rand's reaction nearly made her smile, easing the tension that had grown in her when Gram had introduced the subject.

"That's a lot," she said, her tone milder now.

"And there's a lot to be said for younger men," her grandmother said.

"Gram!" she exclaimed in exaggerated tones. "I'm absolutely shocked!"

"And I'm fifty years married, not dead," her grandmother said, but she was chuckling as she said it.

Impulsively Kate put down the package of spaghetti she'd been putting away and turned to give her grandmother a fierce hug.

"I love you, Gram."

"I love you too, dear. But," she added in an admonishing tone, "you still need to get that life."

Gram was wrong, of course, Kate thought as she headed home. She had a perfectly satisfactory life. And she hadn't really hurried in order to be gone before Rand returned to the house for the evening.

Not much, anyway.

What Gram didn't realize was how hard it really was to resist Rand's charm. It would be hard for any woman, she was sure, but to one who had been alone as long as she had, it was doubly difficult. Why he had set his sights on her she couldn't imagine. There had to be countless women who would adore the attention from him, would love for him to want a relationship. If her life were a little simpler right now, she might actually consider it herself.

But right now she could only hope he gave up before she gave in.

When the phone rang just after midnight, Kate sat up and stared at it for a moment, befuddled. There hadn't been a shipment tonight, so what on earth would someone be calling her at this hour for?

Rubbing at one bleary eye she picked up the handset, looked at the caller ID screen and saw who the call was from. Her heart leaped to her throat in a rush of worry. She pushed the talk button hurriedly.

"Gram? What's wrong?"

"It's Rand."

Kate blinked at the sound of his voice. What was he doing on her grandparents' phone at this hour? And why was he calling her?

"Kate," he said, and she knew from the way he said it she wasn't going to like what was coming next. "We're taking your grandmother to the hospital."

Chapter 12

Kate's stomach plummeted.

"No," she whispered. "Not Gram."

She shivered almost violently at the thought of losing the woman who had raised and taught and loved her.

"Tell me," she said, barely managing to get the words out. Her hand tightened on the phone as she braced herself to hear the worst.

"She's having some chest pains."

Oh, God. "Have you called the paramedics?"

"She wouldn't allow it," he said.

She was tempted to tell him to call them anyway, but she knew her grandmother's stubborn streak.

"And," he added, "I don't think it's that bad, it's already easing, but still it was enough that I don't want to leave it until morning to have her checked."

Kate was too worried to comment on his possessive

words, in fact was glad someone else was there with them. "What about Gramps?"

"He's helping her dress. I'll drive them, if you want to meet us there."

"You know where the hospital is?"

"Roughly, and your grandfather says he can direct me there."

"Yes, yes he can. I'll be right behind you."

She scrambled to dress, slipping on her sheepskin boots and a heavy coat against the cold. She grabbed up her keys and her cell phone and headed for her car at a run. The hospital was forty minutes away at the best of times, and she knew every one of them was going to feel an hour long.

She drove through a night of darkness and cold, but neither could match what she was feeling inside.

"Walter?"

Rand had been watching the older man since they'd arrived at the emergency room. He'd seen the fear and the worry in the man's face, but he also thought he'd seen something more. Knowledge.

"What's wrong, Walt?"

The man finally turned away from the swinging double doors that had separated him from his beloved wife.

"It's that damned angina again."

"Angina?" Rand asked.

"We knew she had it, but she insisted she was fine, it wasn't bad, and that we couldn't afford for her to go on medication," Walt said bitterly.

Rand's gut knotted. He glanced at the double doors himself, wondering if the woman he'd come to like so well would ever come back out.

"Gramps!"

Kate's voice rang out across the lobby of the small emergency room. Rand turned to see her running toward them, her dark hair damp from the moisture in the night air. Worry was clear in her face, and Rand felt the knot in his middle tighten. How had this happened, that he had so quickly come to care about the Crawfords? How had he let it get to the point where just the sight of worry on Kate Crawford's face was enough to make him tense up and feel queasy?

"How is she?"

"We don't know yet," Rand said when Walter seemed unable to speak. "There's a doctor with her now."

Kate went to her grandfather and took his arm. "Come, sit down, Gramps. It will probably be a while before we hear anything."

Walt made a token protest, but then let his granddaughter lead him to one of the two-person couches upholstered in a muted shade of green. They sat, clinging to each other as they awaited word on the most important woman in both their lives. Rand had to turn away as memories assailed him.

Needing to do something, he tracked down a vending machine and bought three cups of coffee. It was barely drinkable, but it was warm, and the cup would heat their hands. They thanked him, but it was automatic; they were both sitting with their attention riveted on those double doors that remained stubbornly closed.

It seemed like hours before a young woman in blue scrubs came through the doors into the waiting room. Both Kate and her grandfather leaped to their feet. The woman smiled and said quickly, "She's fine."

"Thank God," Walt said, while Kate let out a long, relieved sigh.

"I'd like to keep her here until morning, just to make

sure, but it appears it's a flare-up of angina. You knew about that?"

"No," Kate said.

"Yes," her grandfather said, and Kate turned to stare at him.

"You knew she had it?"

Walter looked uncomfortable, but nodded.

"And you never told me?"

"What could you have done?" he asked, then looked back at the doctor. "She's really all right?"

"She will be. But it needs to be addressed. She said she's not on medication?"

"No."

"She'll need to see her own doctor, then, and a cardiologist. Soon. She'd do well on a beta blocker, I think, but that's up to your personal physician."

A grimace flicked across Walter's face, and Rand knew he wouldn't soon forget the look in the older man's eyes. And it wasn't hard for him to guess what inspired the combination of pain and guilt; Dorothy's husband felt like he wasn't properly taking care of his wife.

And right then Rand decided he had to do something about it.

"Sure, darlin', we can do that."

Rand smiled at the easy drawl of Valerie Hill, the head of Redstone's personnel benefits office. The woman was a born-and-bred Texan, and proudly clung to the accent despite over two decades in California.

"Thanks, Val," he said.

"I'll get started on it right away. We should probably be able to pull it together by the weekend."

"Darlin', you are truly a wonder," he said, making her laugh.

His next morning phone call was to his boss to check in. There were several clicks as the call rang through, so he knew something was up. But still, he was surprised when instead of Draven's voice he heard the clipped, brisk tones of St. John, Josh Redstone's right-hand man.

"Draven's on assignment," he was informed. "I'm taking over for him as your contact."

"Okay," Rand said neutrally.

In spite of the fact that the man made him a bit nervous, he was almost relieved; Draven knew him too well, and had noticed his resistance to the idea of Kate as a suspect. St. John, despite being omnipresent at Redstone and seemingly nearly omniscient, wasn't the type to ask bothersome personal questions.

And right now Rand knew he was in big trouble in that particular arena.

"He left some information here for you. I've e-mailed it."

"All right," Rand said, wondering if the answer to his question about Kate's finances was there. And whether he was going to be happy with what it said.

"Anything to report?"

"Not yet. Whoever it is is very good, or on the inside. Or both."

St. John didn't comment. It wasn't necessary, since they both knew Josh would have little mercy on the perpetrator of an inside job.

"Anything else?"

"Ship me out some night-vision binoculars. And I may need that tracking device, but I'll let you know."

"It will be ready."

Rand disconnected and smothered a yawn. He'd awakened early to make his calls, and that, after the late night at the hospital, had left him extra tired. But he had promised Walt he'd drive him to pick up Dorothy so that Kate didn't have to take off work. He glanced at the clock. 8:15 a.m. They'd said she'd be released at eleven. Maybe he could go back to sleep for a couple of hours.

First, he'd check for that e-mail, though. He connected his laptop to the Redstone mainframe and downloaded his e-mail. He was relieved to see the e-mail from St. John was only the report on the kids, Mel and her boyfriend Derek, which held nothing unexpected, just routine teenage difficulties. Nothing about Kate yet at all.

He laid back down on top of the quilt so he wouldn't go to sleep too deeply. At least, that was the theory, but he was quickly asleep, soundly enough to dream. And for the first time in a very long time he dreamed of Donna, and the day she'd walked out of his life, telling him they'd made an awful mistake, trying to base a relationship on the adrenaline-induced attraction they'd developed when he'd pulled her and her daughter out of that African civil war that had broken out while he was there to secure a Redstone airstrip.

Mandy.

Her sweet little face, with those huge chocolate-brown eyes that had burned their way into his heart. He had adored that child, and thought about her every time he saw a blond little girl with brown eyes.

He woke up wishing he'd never tried to sleep. That had been the first time in his life he'd thought himself truly and forever in love. In truth, it had been the only time. It seemed like a lifetime ago. But looking back, he didn't know how much had been real and how much had been the adrenaline of escaping death together. He'd eventually come to realize Donna had likely been right, that there hadn't been enough to build on. But he still missed little Mandy, wondered what she was like now, and if she ever thought of him.

And, he thought as he shook himself awake, he remembered what it had felt like to fall in love. And there was no similarity to whatever he was feeling about Kate Crawford. He wouldn't be that foolish. Surely he wouldn't.

A glance at the clock told him he'd gotten a little over an hour, though, and that was better than nothing. He'd feel better as soon as he shook off the grogginess, he told himself, and sat up to pull on his shoes.

If only he could shake off the lingering images from the unexpected dream as easily.

There were, Kate thought, many reasons for her to feel unsettled, over and above the thefts here at work, which she still had no answer for.

Gram, first of all of course. That had been a scare she could have done without, and learning that they had known of this condition and not told her was even more upsetting. She simply had to find a way to improve her grandparents' financial situation.

Maybe she should move back into her old room at the house. That would save her rent, which, while not huge, would make an immediate difference. She'd miss her little cottage, but nothing was worth the people she loved most doing without the medical care they needed.

Problem was, there was no way she was going to live under the same roof as Rand Singleton. The man was simply too cute, too sexy and too young. The sooner he moved on, the better off she would be. No matter that her grandparents thought he was wonderful, and that she was a fool for not pursuing his interest in her.

He is not, Kate insisted to herself, the reason she was

so unsettled. At least, he wasn't the *only* reason, she amended ruefully.

She let out a heavy sigh. How had the simple life she loved, the life she'd come back home to live, gotten so complicated?

She tried to snap out of it, tried to concentrate on her work. She made several calls, ordered the next quarter's office supplies, requested a quote for having a gasoline tank installed for the delivery trucks and finished her monthly report to her boss. The last one made her wince when she had to include the data on the latest theft and admit they were no closer to solving the mystery of how it was being done than they'd been after the first incident.

When her phone rang, it was a relief.

"Distribution," she said into the receiver.

"Kate? It's Claudia. Got a minute?"

"For you? Sure," she told their in-house personnel director.

"I wanted to let you know about this so you can pass it on to your people. We'll be having the annual health fair next Saturday."

"The health fair?" Kate asked, puzzled.

Every year each Redstone facility set up a day for employees to be tested for various things, or consult with a doctor about things that they had put off, or simply have a basic checkup. And if they then needed a referral to a specialist, that also was handled under the auspices of Redstone's extended health care plan.

"Isn't that normally supposed to be in the spring?" she asked.

"Normally, yes, but it's been rescheduled this year. Actually, they've revamped a lot of things. Including eligibility. It's open to family now."

"Family?" Kate said, sitting up straighter.

"Yes, isn't that wonderful? I'm bringing in my sister, since she's too stubborn to make an actual doctor's appointment for her arthritis."

"Would that include grandparents?" Kate held her breath waiting for the answer.

"Of course. I thought of you and specifically asked."

"Thank you, Claudia. Thank you so much."

As she hung up, Kate was almost shaking with relief. Gram would be able to see the specialist she needed. Bless Josh Redstone.

After that it was with a considerably lighter heart that she turned to the shipping schedule, which included the next shipment of pumps, set to go out in two weeks. And just that quickly the edge was off her improved mood.

For a while she simply sat there looking at the date with dread. That one line on the schedule seemed to pulse, to flicker, as if it were taunting her with the inevitability of yet another loss. She rubbed at her eyes, wondering if she was losing her mind over this.

Shaking her head, she made herself scan the rest of the schedule for the places the updated numbers she had received yesterday afternoon needed to be inserted. After a moment she frowned; she knew she hadn't put that data in, yet there it was. Mel must have done it, she thought. The data had been on her desk. It wasn't as if they could keep the shipment a secret; too many people had to know.

To confirm her suspicions, she called up the stats on the file, and there it was; it had been modified yesterday, about a half an hour after she'd left. She'd have to thank the girl for saving her the twenty or so minutes it took. She went back to the main page and closed the file.

Her finger froze on the mouse button as an image replayed in her head. Slowly she moved the cursor back to the menu and again opened the stats box.

She hadn't been imagining it. She stared at the gray box of details on the file, at the date and time that she had seen without really registering it.

Her stomach began to churn as she acknowledged the reality of what she was seeing. There was no good explanation for what the data on the computer screen was showing her. No innocent explanation.

Mel hadn't just updated the shipping schedule, with the vulnerable shipment on it.

She'd printed it.

Chapter 13

Rand was waiting for her when she got off work. She was startled to see him in the lobby of her building, chatting with the very person she was going to have to confront soon. Mel's hair stripes were orange today, an almost neon shade that made Kate blink.

"Hey, here she is," the girl said.

The look she gave Kate seemed utterly genuine and innocent, as was the grin on her face when she turned her back to Rand and made a wiggling gesture with one hand that Kate recognized as the universal female acknowledgement of a hot guy. She tried to fight down the blush that threatened to heat her cheeks, and the effort made her voice a little gruff when she spoke to the unexpected visitor.

"What are you doing here?" Kate asked boldly.

"Waiting for you," Rand said, unruffled by her tone.

"Why?"

"To take you to dinner. Maybe even a movie."

"Cool!" Mel exclaimed.

"We don't have a theater," Kate pointed out.

Mel rolled her eyes. "So you go to Poulsbo. Duh."

Kate shot a sharp glance at her mentee, hoping she would back off. The girl was all business when working, but once she was through for the day she reverted to pure teenager. The girl seemed oblivious.

"Look," she said to Rand, "I don't have time to—"

"Are you crazy?" Mel said. Then she turned to Rand. "Hey, if she doesn't want to go, I will. I'd love to be seen with a real hottie."

Rand grinned at the girl. "Thanks for the vote."

"Any time." Mel looked him up and down. "Believe me, any time."

"If you two are quite finished?" Kate was irked for reasons she didn't understand.

"That depends," Mel said in arch tones. "On if you're going to be smart and go with him."

"I have to get home and—"

"You have to eat." Rand cut her off smoothly. "And over dinner we can negotiate the rest."

"Perfect," Mel answered, and with a huge grin and a wink at Kate, she added "You two have fun, now." She giggled as she walked away.

For a moment Kate just stared after the girl as she left the building. It just didn't seem possible that that innocent face and manner could be hiding the kind of duplicity that would be necessary for her to be involved in the thefts. Could the girl really be so blasé to her face and be a thief behind her back? And she knew she was avoiding confronting her because she was afraid of the answers she might get.

She turned back to Rand. "Do I need to point out that she's sixteen years old?"

Rand's brow furrowed. "Hardly." Then realization dawned on his face. "Oh, I get it. I'm too young for you, but too old for her. Make up your mind, Kate."

She flushed. It sounded so silly, put like that. But Rand seemed unperturbed, and went on as if they'd not been interrupted.

"How does seafood sound?"

It took her a moment to pull her attention back. "Fine," she said, still absently.

"Good," he said, and took her arm.

She'd just agreed to another dinner with him, she realized. And surprisingly, she didn't feel her usual urge to try and find a way out of it. Maybe it would calm her down, to have to think about something else. Still, she let her earlier thoughts tumble through her head as he walked her toward the visitors' parking area where his car was.

She had thought she would be fixated on her problems the entire evening. Instead, eventually, she found herself actually enjoying the evening. At first she'd only been partially listening to Rand, who was telling her about a photograph he'd taken today of a bald eagle being dive-bombed by a gull with more guts than sense. But as time passed she couldn't help but get involved in the conversation, and at his prompting told him stories of her childhood here, rambling through the woods and the novelty—for him—of finding otters, deer, raccoons and the occasional bear wandering through the yard of her home.

He seemed entranced by her beloved Northwest home, and that was enough to encourage her to share more about this place that she so loved. And she asked him more about his own travels, his family, his life, and he answered her with an easy charm that was very hard to resist.

When she realized that once again she was laughing as often as not, realized that the awful tightness had left her shoulders and the distant throb at her temples had eased, she was amazed.

And then a feeling of impending torment overtook her as she realized that she liked this man, liked him more than she had liked any man she'd met in the years since her marriage had crumbled.

Too cute, too sexy and too young.

The refrain echoed in her head, and she thought she'd be wise to make it a mantra to be repeated regularly in moments like this, moments when she caught herself wondering what it would be like to simply give in to his blandishments and see where it led.

"So tell me, Kate. What is it about me that makes you back off like you just did?"

She nearly gaped at him. And to think most women complained about men being oblivious to emotional undercurrents, she muttered to herself. This wasn't the first time he'd startled her with his perception, but this was the most personal it had gotten. She wasn't sure what to say. And was hideously embarrassed when the only words that popped out of her mouth were the ones she had been chanting to herself almost since she'd first laid eyes on him.

"You're too cute, too sexy and too young."

His expression, telling her that she'd finally taken him off guard, ameliorated her embarrassment a little. That it took him a moment to recover and say anything eased the feeling a little more.

"Uh…thanks?"

That he said it in the tone of a question almost made

her laugh. Again. "I'm sure you've been told that before," she said.

"In fact, I have. Not usually all at once, however. And believe it or not," he added, enunciating with noticeable care, "there are people who find those attributes positive ones."

"My husband was gorgeous and sexy."

"Oh." Understanding flashed across his face in the form of a slight grimace.

"He was also all flash and no substance. No staying power. When the going got tough, he got going—to a divorce lawyer."

He seemed to consider that for a moment. "So, if I went out and got my face bashed in, you'd like me more?"

Again, it sounded ridiculous put that way, which she was sure was what he'd meant to do. "I like you fine," she said. *Too well,* she added silently. "But trusting a pretty face is something else again."

"Trust," he said.

And in that flat, single syllable was an undertone she couldn't quite put a name to. Weariness, perhaps. She didn't think it was bitterness, although there seemed to be a touch of it.

"A precious commodity," she said.

"Can't be bought, except with time."

He sounded, she thought, like a man who didn't have much of that particular currency. She wondered if he sounded that way because he was only here temporarily, or because of something else.

Perhaps he was already making plans to leave, she thought suddenly, and winced inwardly at the pang the thought caused. *Wonderful,* she thought. She was already feeling the pinch of his inevitable departure, despite all her efforts to hold her emotions at bay. She barely knew him, yet she was missing him before he even left.

It sounded as neurotic as she was feeling just now.

Rand tugged the collar of his jacket closed against the chilly air. Kate seemed unaffected by the temperature as they walked back to her car. Her coat was heavy, but left unbuttoned, and she didn't seem to notice.

The Redstone parking lot was empty except for her car and two others, an older compact and a minivan of fairly recent vintage.

"People working late?" he asked casually.

She glanced in the direction he'd been looking. "Security, and the van is the shop's. The night mechanic drives it," she said.

He'd known the older car belonged to the young security guard, but hadn't seen the mechanic drive that van before. He wondered if there was any way to ask about it without rousing her suspicions.

"Family man, huh? Minivans and kids," he said, making it sound like the typical observation of a single guy looking at a man whose free life had ended.

"It's his wife's," Kate acknowledged. "But Ray says they're getting rid of it as soon as the last kid graduates."

Rand smiled. "Ah, the blessings of the empty nest, as my parents have often said."

She smiled back, and he was startled at the jolt of warmth that shot through him. "I think I'd like your parents," she said.

"Yes, I think you would," he said, meaning it. "And they'd like you, too. They have a soft spot for gutsy, smart, compassionate people."

She blinked. "That was…quite a compliment."

He grinned. "I figure you probably get complimented on your looks all the time, so I thought I'd go for the rest of the package."

"And so," she said, one corner of her mouth quirking upward, "was that."

His grin widened. "Like I said, smart."

"No wonder Gram likes you," she said.

"I like her," he said. "And your grandfather. Underneath all that gruffness, he's a sweetheart."

"Yes, he is," Kate said, and the love that echoed in her voice made him, once more, want to call his parents and thank them for being who they were.

He stood by as she unlocked her car, then pulled open the driver's door for her. She leaned over to toss in her purse. He took a step closer, so that when she straightened up again, they were mere inches apart.

"Thank you for dinner," she said, and he noted with satisfaction that her voice was the tiniest bit breathless.

"My pleasure," he said, leaning closer.

She looked up at him, her eyes widening. But she didn't pull away, didn't voice a protest, didn't do any of the things to stop him that he'd half expected.

He barely brushed her lips with his, but still she was as sweet and warm as he'd imagined. And he'd imagined a lot. He went back for more, and then more, because he couldn't stop himself, and this time he was determined to taste her thoroughly. Her mouth was soft and pliant beneath his, and he didn't sense any resistance from her, despite her earlier explanations of her reluctance.

And then rational thought fled, and all he could think about was the feel and taste of her—and his body's fierce, sudden response. She gave out a small, whimpering sound that made his muscles tighten involuntarily. He pulled her closer, pressing the length of her against him, not caring if the movement betrayed how instantly and completely she'd aroused him.

He probed with his tongue, and when her lips parted to admit him, a rush of heat careened through him with a force that nearly staggered him. He realized then that her arms were around his neck, and that she wasn't very steady on her feet herself. And he made himself break the kiss before they both slid to the cold ground beneath their feet.

For a long, silent moment, in the golden halo of the parking lot light, they just stared at each other. He saw her swallow, then she moved a hand to touch her lips with her fingers, her gaze never leaving his face.

"Wow," she finally said, her voice sounding as wobbly as he was feeling.

"Yeah," he agreed, a little shaken himself. "Good thing it's cold out."

She lowered her gaze then, and he knew she'd felt the same blast of heat he had. Quickly, as if she were anxious to get away from him, she turned to get into her car. He let her, but before he closed the door he leaned down.

"We started a fire, Kate. Don't snuff it out before you give it a chance."

The metaphor was a bit mangled, but he knew from the quick, wary glance she gave him that she'd gotten his point. And that she had indeed been thinking this was a flame that needed to be extinguished before somebody got burned.

And as he straightened up and watched her drive out of the Redstone lot, he couldn't deny that he understood just how she felt. And he had the thought that when she found out who he really was, that just might do it.

Chapter 14

Kate awoke fired with a new determination. She was going to focus solely on this mess at work until it was resolved. She would work as long as it took today to get ahead, then she would do nothing but work on the mystery of the thefts. It should have been her top priority all along, she told herself.

And the fact that concentrating fully on the thefts would leave her little time to think about a certain baby-faced boarder was an advantage.

A shiver went through her as she got into the shower. It had nothing to do with the growing morning chill of the season, and everything to do with memories of a kiss. A kiss that had nearly knocked her out of her sheepskin boots.

The warm water pouring over her was welcome, yet unsettling. It was as if the touch of Rand's mouth on hers had revved up her body, and now, hours later, it was still humming. Even the touch of the water was different; she was more aware of the wet heat as it poured over her, more aware of her own skin, too aware of the nerve endings just beneath the surface.

It wasn't fair. No single kiss should have that effect. That a few moments of bodily contact could turn her world upside down was something she wasn't ready to deal with. It had never happened to her before, and the only thing she could think of to do was ignore it.

Too bad her body wasn't cooperating with the game plan.

She needed to get to the office, she thought. There, with other people around and the distractions of work and noise and conversations, she could put this out of her mind. She began to hurry, toweling off and dressing as quickly as she could manage, smothering her irritation at the extra drag of trying to slip clothes over damp skin.

Once she was in her car and moving, she began to feel less rattled. She focused on driving as if she were a teenager with her first license, the running commentary in her mind serving well to keep out other thoughts. Eventually she knew she'd have to deal with it, but not now.

Usually it took her several minutes to get from the doors to her lobby, since people always stopped her en route to talk. Today, since she was a bit early, she saw no one.

Figures, she muttered to herself. *The one day I'd welcome the interruptions, and nobody's around.*

She stepped into her office, dropped her purse in the desk drawer, and reached over to turn on her computer. While it was booting up she checked her in-basket for anything that might have been dropped off. The only thing there was a memo from her boss asking for an update on the status of the theft situation.

"I wish I had something to update you on," she said to the memo form.

When the computer was ready she checked her e-mail. Nothing unusual there, although a note from Mel caught her eye. She opened it, read it and felt a sudden rush of relief that she hadn't jumped on the girl about having printed the shipping schedule. She had done it, the e-mail said, so she could set up the next spreadsheet ahead of time, giving them a head-start on the monthly distribution report.

"That's what you get for being so suspicious," she told herself.

Assuming, of course, the note was the truth, and not just a clever ploy to throw off suspicion.

The sudden thought made her frown, both at the possibility of it being true and the fact that she'd become so mistrusting that it had occurred to her at all. But from now on, no matter how difficult it made things, she was going to restrict access to the schedule. But it seemed she had no choice in the matter; until this was resolved, she had no choice but to be suspicious of anything that could be connected, even remotely.

That fact made another decision for her. She reached for the phone, her finger hovering over the speed dial button that would connect her to Redstone Headquarters. Then she hesitated.

Coward, she chided herself. But she pushed an extension number instead.

On the second ring she heard a rustling and then a cheery "Hello?"

"Brian, it's Kate."

"Hi, Ms. Crawford," Brian Fisher said.

She'd tried repeatedly to get the young security guard to call her Kate, but he persisted in the formality. It made her feel old, as if he'd been taught by his mother how to properly address his elders, and that she was definitely in that category, at least in his view.

"I've been thinking that we should go ahead and get that surveillance system."

"We're sure not having much luck without it."

The young man had been all in favor of having the cameras and monitors installed when the facility first opened. Kate hoped they wouldn't need anything like that here in Summer Harbor, but ultimately her boss decided they'd wait until the new system they'd been told about was available, the more efficient one that was motion activated.

"Why don't you go ahead and arrange for it?"

"You bet," he said eagerly. "I'll call right away."

They talked about the logistics for a few minutes, then she hung up, satisfied. She knew that anyone who was hired in any security capacity for Redstone underwent an extensive background investigation, so she had little worry about entrusting Brian with this information. And he was new enough at his work to need some bolstering, and entrusting him with this project should help there, too.

She smiled, as she always did when her good fortune was brought home to her; working for Redstone was indeed a pleasure. They were even going to help her take care of her grandparents, and she doubted there were many companies in the world who would do that.

She had to fix this. She owed Redstone so much. She wanted to justify Josh Redstone's trust in her. She felt like she was personally letting him and the company down, and it gnawed at her. She'd never felt this way about anywhere she'd worked. Belonging to the Redstone family had responsibilities as well as huge benefits. She had to—

Her phone rang. The display indicated an inside call, so she answered it quickly.

"Ms. Crawford? It's Brian. I had a question."

"Problem with getting the system?"

"No, not at all. It's on its way, should be here in a couple of days. But…"

He hesitated, uncertainty in his voice. He was, she thought, so young. Which made her think of Rand.

"What is it?" she prompted, trying to put an encouraging note in her voice.

"I was wondering. Are you going to tell anyone the cameras are there? Or keep it quiet?"

She'd been thinking about that decision she'd have to make soon. If she made some sort of announcement, perhaps the thefts would simply stop. That would solve the problem. But it wouldn't tell them how it was being done, and who on the inside was possibly involved.

She had a feeling she knew what Josh Redstone would want. His reputation was well known among his people. He would go to the wall to protect his own, but she also knew he had a low tolerance for bad apples in his own bunch. He would want to weed out this one.

And what if it really was Mel?

Kate sighed. She truly didn't want to believe that. True, there had been an innocent explanation for everything she'd caught her doing, but there was a guilty one as well. And whoever was doing this was obviously clever enough to throw off suspicion.

"Ms. Crawford?"

Brian's query brought her out of her troubled thoughts. "For now, let's keep it quiet," she said. She could announce it later if need be, but once that bird had flown, there was no calling it back.

"Okay," Brian said, obviously pleased by her answer.

"You'd like to catch someone, wouldn't you?"

"Yes, ma'am," he exclaimed. The "ma'am" made her feel positively creaky. "I'd sure like to. Mr. Redstone, he took a chance hiring me when I had no experience, and I'd like to pay him back."

"I know the feeling," Kate said. "We're going to solve this, Brian."

He responded to the "we" as she'd hoped. If he'd been in uniform, he probably would have saluted.

"Yes, ma'am!"

So now, all she had to do was wait for the equipment. And think. She wasn't sure what she could possibly come up with after weeks of fruitless pondering. She only knew she had to try.

Rand waited a good half hour after Kate turned up her gravel driveway before he followed. He didn't want her to figure out that he'd been following her. But he wasn't sure how much longer he could hide the fact. She was hardly a stupid woman; sooner or later she was going to notice the frequency with which she saw his vehicle.

Especially now that she'd been in it a couple of times; it was human nature to notice cars that people you knew drove. It was why once a friend bought a particular model, you suddenly saw them everywhere. They'd always been there, but you never noticed before because there was no personal connection.

Personal connection.

He let out a long breath. He'd spent hours trying to pry her out of his mind, lecturing himself on staying professional. He dredged up the old pain of Donna's desertion with Mandy, warned himself that that was what happened if you got involved on a case. It was just asking for disaster.

But that brought to mind what had happened to Sam when she had crossed that line.

And it wasn't that he had anything against marriage. Quite the opposite. He'd had a great example in the relationship his parents had, and always figured he'd end up there someday. He even knew that he'd like kids, a couple maybe. Mandy had convinced him of that.

He'd also, somewhat arrogantly he supposed, assumed that when he found the right woman, it would be mutual. He never expected he would have to convince, persuade and coerce to get close.

When he realized he was thinking of Kate as that "right" woman, he nearly slammed on his brakes. Lord, was he that far gone already? He didn't make a habit out of thinking about marriage and kids for no reason. Of course, that toe-curling, sock-shedding kiss could hardly be classified as "no reason." And it seemed that kiss had awakened a lot more than just nerve endings.

Rattled, he considered turning around and, as Sam Gamble's little brother would say, "beating feet." He wasn't even sure why he didn't, although he was honest enough not to tell himself it was only because of the job he had yet to finish.

When he pulled up to the house, he saw a light on in the back. Grabbing the bag from the seat beside him, he got out, ran up the three front steps and knocked on the door.

It took her a couple of minutes to get there, and when she opened the door she was tugging at the hem of a soft, gold sweater she must have just pulled on. He determinedly steered his mind away from visions of Kate undressing, and smiled at her.

"Hi."

There was a moment's hesitation, and he thought he saw a trace of color rise in her cheeks. That tiny sign that she wasn't indifferent pleased him enormously, but even as he realized that fact, she had herself back in control.

"Hello," she said, just the slightest bit of puzzlement in her voice, as if at his unexpected appearance.

He grinned as he held up the plastic bag. "Help. I was caught by the lure of fresh salmon."

Her expression cleared and after a moment, a glint of humor appeared in her eyes. "Fresh salmon is a powerful lure," she said, and as if to prove it, she stepped back and gestured him inside.

"So I discovered," he said as he stepped into the house he'd only observed from the outside until now. "Problem is, I don't have a clue how to cook it."

She laughed. "Culinarily challenged, are we?"

"Only when it comes to fish. I can whip you up a mean lemon chicken or some great garlic roasted pork chops, and just about anything else. I can even bake bread. But somehow I never got the fish knack."

While he was talking he was looking around as much as he could without being too obvious. Her home was cozy, warm and everything he'd expected it would be. But there were surprises as well, such as the free-form glass sculpture on an illuminated pedestal, and the rough-textured, jewel-toned weaving that covered a large part of one wall above the big, dark green sofa.

"A man who cooks," she said with a dramatic sigh. "Be still my heart."

"Thank my mother," he said. "She made sure I knew my way around the kitchen. She hated to cook, and as far as she was concerned, the sooner we kids could take over, the better."

"And did you?"

"We did. The deal was if we cooked, we never had to clean up after. Seemed like a cheap way to avoid washing dishes."

She smiled again. "Now I'm sure I'd like your mother."

Rand had a sudden, unexpected vision of Kate and his mom, giggling away like schoolgirls in the kitchen of the house where he'd grown up. It was crazy, they didn't even live in that house anymore, but there it was.

"That must have been an interesting thought."

Rand snapped back to his present surroundings, not even wanting to think about what his expression must have been to prompt that remark.

"Just thinking about my mom," he said quickly, telling himself it wasn't a total lie. But the quick smile she gave him made him feel slightly uncomfortable, as if he'd tried to manipulate her and had succeeded.

Stupid, he muttered to himself. *Your job is manipulation half the time. Get back to business.*

"Let me see what I've got," she said, heading toward what he assumed was the kitchen.

He followed, but slowly, still looking around. The large armoire in the corner of the living room likely housed the television and stereo, if she had them, and he made a mental note to check at the first opportunity, see if any of them were particularly new or cutting edge or both.

The kitchen, when he finally arrived there, was small but as warm and welcoming as the rest of the house. The cabinets were white, the counters covered in colorful tile in greens of various shades, and the centerpiece was a pot rack adorned with gleaming copper pots and pans. The refrigerator was white, while the other appliances had black glass fronts, and none of them looked brand-new.

So, she hasn't remodeled the kitchen lately, he thought, quashing the unrest that rose within him as he made himself look for signs of a recent jump in discretionary cash.

"I think I have a cedar plank here somewhere," she said.

"A cedar plank?"

He'd heard of cooking fish that way, but at the moment he couldn't remember where. Which might have something to do with the fact that Kate had just bent to dig into a lower cupboard, and the sight of her trim, denim clad backside was making his fingers curl.

"Yes," she said, her voice muffled because she was reaching to the back of the shelf. "It comes out great if you grill it on the plank, with butter and dill."

She hadn't, he found later, exaggerated. The rich, buttery salmon steak was beyond delicious. The crusty French bread he recognized from his trips to Turner's grocery store, and was from a local bakery who clearly had the knack. She'd also steamed some fresh green beans and tossed them with some oil and vinegar and spices that he was going to ask her about, since they tasted so good.

And for a while, just for now, he almost managed to put out of his mind why he was here and simply enjoy an evening with a beautiful woman he was greatly attracted to.

He was pleased when Kate also seemed to relax, and the edginess he'd grown to expect in her seemed to fade. Maybe she was becoming more comfortable with him at last.

Or maybe it's the wine, he thought wryly, as she poured them both a second glass of the smoky Oregon pinot noir.

Whatever it was, she did relax enough to tell him some stories about her times in big corporate America. Some of them she told with amusement at decisions that backfired in unexpectedly funny ways, such as the company that chose a name for a product to market in Japan, without realizing that the name sounded very much like the Japanese term for broken. Some tales were tinged with exasperation and frustration at the still solid presence of a glass ceiling for too many women, and how hard she herself had had to fight to get past it.

No wonder you love Redstone, Rand thought. The only ceiling there was the limitation of your own ability.

"Do you regret leaving? That world, I mean?" he asked her as he rose to help her clear the table.

"No." She said it quickly, and with no undertone of doubt or second guessing. "I realized that the money wasn't worth being miserable for."

Then it couldn't be worth it to her to steal, could it?

The swiftness with which the hope rose in him at his own thought rattled him. He was beginning to question his ability to remain impartial about her. Hell, he was beginning to wonder if he had ever been impartial. And that way lay disaster, for his work. He might start looking for evidence to prove her innocent, rather than focusing on evidence to lead him to the culprit, whoever it might be.

She looked at him curiously and he realized he'd been silent too long. He put the plate he'd been rinsing into the dishwasher and said the first thing that popped into his head. "I thought Redstone paid well."

"They do. Very well. But I was making a *lot* of money."

Get to work, he told himself. "It must hard after you've gotten used to being well off."

"I'm doing fine," she said, a bit vehemently. "I just worry about Gram and Gramps. I can't help them as much as I used to, as much as I want to."

"They already feel you do too much for them," he said.

"I could never, ever do too much for them."

She stood there, looking up at him, the light of pure determination in her eyes. And in that moment, he could no more stop himself from kissing her than he could have stopped breathing.

The moment his mouth touched hers he felt her go tense against him. But she didn't push him away, didn't pull away herself, and he felt a flash of relief since he was half convinced he was already beyond stopping anyway. He'd never in his life had anything hit him as hard and fast as the taste of Kate Crawford.

And then she was kissing him back, tentatively. He wondered briefly if she was mentally resisting, or was simply uncertain. He hoped it was the latter. He was about to start praying it was the latter.

He felt her tongue flick over his lips, and a fierce heat shot through him. He leaned into her, putting his hands on the counter on either side of her. It wasn't because he wanted to hem her in, but because he needed the support himself. And, he didn't quite trust his hands not to follow his body's urging to speed things up here.

He felt her hands slip around his neck, felt her fingers thread through his hair. He deepened the kiss, probing, tasting, until he could feel his pulse hammering in his ears. He leaned harder against her, feeling the softness of her breasts pushing against his chest. His fingers curled against the tile of the counter, trying to dig through the ceramic as if it were still unfired clay.

Then he lost the battle and one hand slipped to her waist and slowly, gently stroked upward. He reached the curve of her breast and cupped it. His fingers nearly shook with the effort to be gentle when his body was screaming at him that it wanted this woman *now*.

He rubbed his thumb over the peak of her breast, felt a another rush of heat as it hardened in response. Then she made a tiny sound, deep in her throat, a needy, wanting sound that sliced through him.

He knew he was on the edge of careening out of control. With a wrenching effort he broke off the kiss and took a step back. Or tried to; his legs were none too steady. The fact that Kate seemed to sway slightly, and reached for the counter for support, heartened him. This white hot was not something he wanted to be in alone.

It wasn't until much later that he realized he hadn't even thought that he shouldn't be in it at all.

Chapter 15

She was crazy. There was no other explanation. She simply had to be crazy. It was that or stupid, and she knew that didn't apply. Of course, an IQ well above average didn't necessarily mean you had any sense, as Gramps always said.

And she clearly had no sense at all. None. Why else would she be sitting here on her porch on a sunny Sunday morning, letting her imagination run away with her? Letting the memory of last night overtake her, stopping her breath all over again, and making her heart speed up and her body heat at the thought of what might have happened if he hadn't stopped.

But he had stopped. It had only been a kiss. He'd kissed her, that's all. So what?

Okay, so he'd kissed her twice now. And both times sent her spinning into a realm of sensations she'd never visited before. So what? It didn't make him any older, or her any younger. It didn't change that he didn't seem to ever stay in one place for long. It didn't change that she wasn't ready for any kind of relationship, and wasn't the type for a casual fling. It didn't change that she was buried in debt and he, judging by the things she'd noticed, was likely better than well off.

So what? she told herself again.

Maybe, if she repeated it often enough, she might even believe it.

She realized she was hugging herself, both her arms tense and tight. No wonder, since she felt as if she was about to fly apart.

Nothing had changed. The sooner Rand Singleton moved on, the better off she was going to be. That was the bottom line, and she'd better remember it. It didn't matter what his kiss did to her, didn't matter that she spent far too much time thinking about him. It also didn't matter that her grandmother kept touting him, telling Kate what a great guy he was, and that she'd be a fool to let him get away.

No, the longer he stayed, the more attached she would become, and the more it would hurt in the end, when he finally did leave.

Forcing herself to abandon the futile pondering, she tried to decide what to do today. She thought about going in to work, but she had put in so many hours already this week that she couldn't quite face that. There had to be other things around here that needed doing. She'd paid bills this morning. She'd done laundry yesterday, had just finished when Rand had arrived—

Stop it, she told herself.

What else? She'd vacuumed two days ago. She needed

to run the dishwasher after last night's dinner; she'd been too rattled after Rand had kissed her to—

Stop it!

There was some gardening she could do, she thought. That might be just the ticket. Get her hands dirty, dig, weed, whack away at some ubiquitous berry bushes, see some meaningful progress.

Progress. Now that would be a nice change, she told herself. Decision made, she went inside to change clothes. It was still a bit brisk, but she knew she'd soon be too warm for a sweatshirt so she pulled out a T-shirt to put on underneath. Next came the freshly laundered, faded and garden-stained jeans she usually wore, and a scrunchie to pull her hair back out of her face.

She grabbed a bottle of water from the fridge and went back outside. She opened the storage bench she kept on the front porch, pulled out her perpetually muddy rubber boots, her gloves, and her bucket of tools. Geared up, she was ready to start.

It took effort, but she managed to keep her mind on what she was doing most of the time. She'd decided to tackle the encroaching blackberry canes first, since she had to watch what she was doing to avoid the thorns. Not that she was completely successful; as usual she was bleeding from several scratches before she was through. She'd also worked up a sweat despite the fact that it was only sixty degrees out, and had managed to get smears of dirt on her face as she pulled off the now too-warm sweatshirt.

She reached into the bucket for the bottle of water. She took a long swig, then closed the top and turned to drop it back in the tool bucket. In the instant after the bottle left her fingers, she caught movement at the periphery of her vision. She glanced that way. And froze.

A car was pulling into her driveway. Not just any car. Rand's car.

Her first reaction was so classically female she almost laughed at herself; all she could think of was that she was a complete mess.

Well, this may just solve your problem, she thought with an inward chuckle. *He'll take one look at this and turn tail as fast as he can.*

He stopped in her driveway when he saw her out by the berry patch. She turned then, figuring she might as well give him the full picture of her disarray. He got out of the car and started toward her, carrying a flat package wrapped in green paper.

You are not *going to apologize for how you look,* she ordered herself sternly.

As it turned out, she didn't have a chance to anyway.

"I'm glad you're here," Rand said, smiling as he approached, smiling as if he didn't even notice she was sweaty and dirty and clad in her grubbiest clothes. "I wanted to— You're bleeding!"

He shoved the package under his arm to hold it and grabbed for both her hands, apparently heedless of how dirty her gardening gloves where. He turned her arms to better see the angry marks.

"Just scratches from the berries," she said with a shrug. "It comes with the territory."

He frowned, glanced at the bushes as if he were contemplating mayhem, then back at her. "You should have somebody do that."

"I don't mind. It satisfies my need to do battle with something."

He raised a brow at her. "Feeling a bit militant today?"

"Maybe."

He looked at her steadily for a silent moment. When he finally spoke, his voice was soft, rueful.

"Did you have as rough a night as I did?"

Suddenly she was glad for the dirt on her face; at least she could hope it hid her blush.

"Salmon didn't agree with you?" She knew she was dissembling, but she had no idea what else to say.

"The salmon was wonderful," he said, never moving his gaze from her face. "And so was everything else."

She thought about pretending she had no idea what he meant, but couldn't quite bring herself to do it.

"Yes," she said softly. "It was."

She heard him let out a long breath, as if of relief. "I was awake all night, wanting more. Much more."

She remembered her own restless night, and felt her warm cheeks grow warmer. She was afraid he was going to pursue it, and right now she couldn't think of anything she wanted less. But he didn't. Instead he held out the package he carried.

"I wanted to thank you for dinner."

"You brought it," she protested.

"That was the easy part." He gestured at the package. "I hope you like it."

"I…thank you." She tugged off her gloves, dusted her hands off as best she could, and took the package. It was a box about shirt-sized, but heavier. She got the wrapping off and lifted the lid. Her breath caught.

"I thought about flowers, but…" His voice trailed off as if he were uncertain about the reception his offering was going to get.

"No," she whispered, staring down at the silver-framed portrait of her grandparents. "No, this is so much better."

She looked up at him, even knowing her eyes were

brimming. He deserved to know how much this meant to her. And the smile he gave her told her she'd been right about his uncertainty.

"You captured them," she said. "The softness behind Gramps's curmudgeonly exterior, and the humor and sparkle in Gram's eyes. It's all here. Thank you, Rand."

"You're welcome. I just snapped off the shot one morning when they were sitting out on the deck. I didn't realize what I had until I saw the print."

That he had realized at all told her a lot about him. Not everyone had that kind of perceptiveness. "It's wonderful. I love it."

"I'm glad." He glanced over her shoulder. "Now, why don't I help you finish that?"

"Oh, no, it's an awful job, you don't have to—"

"Please. I want to. On one condition."

"What's that?"

"No more bloodshed," he said, looking at her scratched arms.

"I'm all for that," she said ruefully.

He pulled off his jacket, clearly ready to dive in and get started. She couldn't think of a reason to stop him, and if she was honest about it, she didn't want to.

With his help, the job was done in a fraction of the time it would have taken her. And he managed to escape any major encounters with the thorns, except for an occasional puncture that had him saying he would never eat another slice of blackberry pie.

"Speaking of pie," she said, pushing an errant lock of hair behind her ear, "now that you've worked so hard, the least I can do is feed you lunch."

"Now that's an offer I can't refuse."

"Well, it might be. All I've got at the moment is some

leftover meat loaf Gram sent home with me. I was thinking sandwiches."

"One of my favorites," he said with another of those smiles that sent her heart into overdrive.

"Let me just clean up, then." She was proud of how level her voice was.

"You're fine," he said.

She gave him a sideways look. "If that means grubby," she said wryly.

"Functional," he said. "Now, if you'd been out here gardening in an evening gown, you'd still look great but I'd be questioning your common sense."

And that, she thought, was as neat a compliment as she'd ever gotten. This man was beyond dangerous. He was also too, too tempting. And her resistance to that temptation was wavering.

"Thank you," she said, not knowing what else to say.

She picked up the photograph with care not to smudge the glass. Rand tossed the pruners into the tool bucket and picked it up. She showed him where it went, tugged off her gardening boots and led the way inside.

She set the photo down on her small dining table. "I want to think about the perfect place for it. Someplace where I'll be sure and see it every day."

"I'm really glad you like it."

Lord, another smile, she thought. *You'd better get out of here while you still can.* "I'll just take a quick shower," she said.

"Why don't I make the sandwiches while you do?"

She had the unexpected thought that her ex-husband Dan would never in his life have offered to do that. But then, he wouldn't have gotten down and dirty with a Himalayan blackberry bush, either.

"Okay. Bread's on the counter, condiments on the refrigerator door."

"Got it," he said cheerfully and ambled off toward the kitchen. The moment he was out of sight, Kate took a deep breath to steady herself. She felt like she had on her one and only attempt at skiing—as if she were slipping out of control down a steep slope and picking up speed fast.

She had just pulled her jeans and shirt off and tossed them in the laundry basket in her closet when the phone rang. She picked up the cordless to answer and continued to the master bath.

"Katy?"

"Hi, Gram. How are you? No more pains?"

"For the third time today, I'm fine. Did he give it to you?"

"The photo? Yes, he did. I love it. It's perfect."

"He is good, isn't he?"

In more ways than one, Kate thought. "Yes, he is."

"So don't blow it."

"Excuse me?" she asked, startled.

"He's interested, and no woman in her right mind wouldn't be interested right back. You're no fool, Katy girl, don't act like one."

Her grandmother's words echoed in her mind as she got into the shower. She'd finally had to admit to herself that Gram was right, that after Dan she was more than a little wary. And she didn't like the idea that her ex still had any kind of power over her.

So, what do I do about it? she asked herself as she scrubbed her face. *Have a blazing affair with Rand?*

The blast of heat that rocketed through her at just the thought of a blazing affair with Rand Singleton made her stomach turn over. She just stood there for a moment, water pelting her, stunned at her involuntary reaction.

Then soap ran into her eyes and the sting got her moving again. She rinsed it away, hastened through the rest of her shower, quickly toweled off and headed for her closet.

Somehow she doubted choosing what to wear was going to distract her.

Something had changed.

Rand wasn't sure what it was, but he was positive something had. Had the photograph been the key to getting her to trust him? He'd thought it might be, given how she felt about her grandparents. He hadn't expected anything to happen so fast, but he couldn't deny she had changed. It wasn't so much that she'd relaxed around him, but the edginess he sensed now was a new, different kind of tension.

He'd been surprised but pleased when she'd quickly said yes when he asked her out to dinner that night. He'd half expected her to fend him off as she had been doing the past couple of times. He thought about asking her why the change, then quickly decided that was one of the more stupid things he'd ever thought of. Especially when she was being more open and encouraging than she had ever been with him before.

He wanted more than anything to push completely out of his mind the real reason he was in Summer Harbor. Wanted to accept her apparent change of heart at face value. But his first loyalty had to be to Redstone. *Had to be.*

So when he took her home and walked her to the door he opened the subject. "I'm sorry you have to go back to work in the morning."

"Me, too," she said, rather breathlessly.

Something in the way she looked at him made his next breath die in his throat. Only then did he realize how what he'd said could be interpreted in more than one way. And which way she'd taken it.

"Kate." His voice was tight, all thought of his job driven from his mind by the look in her eyes.

Slowly, so slowly he hardly dared to breathe at all, she lifted her arms. Her hands slipped around his neck in an invitation that was unmistakable.

And in his case, irrefusable.

He lowered his head, knowing he was likely going to regret this. But he was unable to stop, because he also knew he'd regret that even more.

This time, she kissed him back wholeheartedly. And he was stunned at the difference her full participation made. Kissing her had been hot before, but this, this was an inferno. And his body's response was so swift he nearly staggered. It was all he could do to break the kiss before he went up in flames.

"Take it easy on me, woman," he said hoarsely, "before I start hearing offers you're not making."

"As long as you hear the one I am making."

For a moment he just stood there stupidly, playing back what she'd said in his mind to be sure he'd heard it right.

"Kate, I didn't mean—"

"I know," she said. "But I did. I don't have to get up *that* early." She drew back slightly. "Unless…you've changed your mind?"

"Not on your life." The words came instantly, before he even thought. Then, when he did think, he had to add, "But I'm not…prepared for this. I don't have anything."

"That's okay. I do." She lowered her gaze, and he knew he wasn't mistaken about the blush. "Of course, I drove forty miles to get them."

Rand just looked at her for a moment, contemplating the

wealth of information that statement had given him. That she was afraid if she'd bought condoms here, everybody in town would know before the day was over, which meant she didn't want to advertise their relationship.

On the other hand, it had clearly been a conscious decision on her part. He knew she wasn't the type to do this casually. She'd thought about it, thought about him, and decided she wanted him. Despite all the obstacles she'd talked about, despite whatever scars her ex had left her with, she wanted him. That took his breath away all over again. And he knew there was no way he could walk away from her.

So why the hell are you standing here analyzing this, instead of kissing her again?

And then he did just that.

Chapter 16

Kate had wondered if she would have second thoughts. Had almost expected to, had expected to panic at the last second, wonder if she wasn't making a huge mistake.

She'd done none of those.

If she was making a mistake, she thought, at least she was doing it with full intention and full speed ahead. But as she stood beside her bed, the bed where she was about to take this irrevocable step, she didn't think it was a mistake. How could anything that felt like this be a mistake?

No, she was right to have taken this chance. No matter what happened, every woman should feel like this at least once. Wherever he touched her her skin tingled. His mouth on hers made her weak in the knees. It was all she could do to keep standing while they wrestled with their clothes.

She knew there would be awkward moments. Like now, when they both stood naked, with nothing to do but look.

Or look away. *But if you feel the need to look away, you probably shouldn't be doing this anyway,* her inner voice reasoned.

And besides, if you have something as beautiful as Rand Singleton in front of you, you should enjoy it.

She felt heat rise in her cheeks at her own thoughts. But it was true, he was beautiful. Tall and strong, but lean, not burly; fit, not muscle-bound. And so potently aroused she felt a shiver inside, and a burst of female power she hadn't felt in a very long time.

A qualm struck her as she wondered how her eight-years-older body would stand up to the kind of scrutiny she was giving him. But he wasn't stupid, he knew how old she was, and she wasn't in bad shape anyway. And obviously— very obviously—he didn't find her particularly lacking.

"Kate," he whispered, reaching for her. She saw his fingers trembling, and the last of her reservations vanished.

He picked her up, easily. Her breath caught; he was even stronger than he looked, because she was not a featherweight. He put her down on the bed with a care that bordered on reverence. For a moment she looked up at him, at the silky hair that persisted in falling over his forehead like a boy's, the blue eyes that were looking at her in a way no boy ever could. Looking at her with such heat and passion that another shiver rippled through her.

He came down beside her in a rush, and a burst of heat shot through her at the touch of his body against hers, skin to skin. His mouth came down on hers once more, fiercely, and she felt her belly clench and ripple under the sweet onslaught. His hands stroked over her until she couldn't stay still; she rose to him as if he were some mythical creature with magic powers. There was no holding back, she wanted his touch everywhere.

He seemed to hesitate for a moment, his hand on her rib cage, just below her breasts.

"Please," she whispered, arching her back, offering them to him.

He growled something that could have been her name, and then his hands moved upward, cupping her, caressing her, then stroking her nipples until they hardened and she gasped at the sheer force of the sensation. At the same time he trailed a burning path of kisses down her throat, and just when she thought she couldn't bear any more, he replaced his fingers with his mouth. The wet heat and the flick of his tongue over already taut flesh made her cry out again, in a wild voice she barely recognized as her own.

For a moment he moved away, and she realized he was reaching for the packet on the nightstand.

"If I don't do this now," he said, catching her glance, "you'll have me so crazy I'll forget to do it at all."

She felt that jolt of feminine power once more at his words. She watched him as he sheathed himself. It had been so very long for her. She had never really known what she was waiting for, except something more than the perfunctory sex she and Dan had had at the end. She had nearly given up on finding it, whatever it was. Perhaps because it had never crossed her path before. Until now.

And now she was tired of waiting.

"I'll try to go slow," he said as he came back to her, "but I can't promise."

"Don't," she said, reaching for him. His skin was sleek and hot beneath her fingers. "Don't go slow."

He groaned in answer and moved over her. For a moment she savored the weight and feel of him, but then even that wasn't enough. Her hands slid down his back to his hips, urging him forward. He fumbled for a moment, which in an odd way excited her more than practiced ease would have. She reached to guide him, loving the sound he made as her fingers touched rigid flesh.

This was it, she thought. This was what she'd been waiting for.

Or who.

A gasp broke from her as he slid forward, stretching her, filling her. He hesitated, and in a convulsive movement she lifted her hips, driving him home. Her name burst from him, and she felt a shudder go through him. His response sent her own senses spiraling upward, and when he began to move, to withdraw and drive forward with a fierce urgency, she could only grab his shoulders and hang on.

She thought she couldn't bear any more, couldn't take any more, and then he shifted position until his every stroke caressed her in a way that made her cry out at the building sensations. He kept on and on until she could barely breathe as her body began to clench.

"Kate," he said, his voice low and harsh. "Kate, I can't—"

His words stopped on a guttural sound that she felt begin deep in his chest. His hands slid to her shoulders, to hold her as he slammed into her one last time. Her body convulsed and she moaned his name as he sent her flying.

Kate's amused, sensual laugh lingered in Rand's mind as he crept up the stairs of the Crawford house as quietly as he could. He hadn't wanted to leave her, but Walt and Dorothy knew he was taking their granddaughter out tonight, and while getting home late was one thing, not coming home at all was something else entirely.

He'd been worried about her reaction when he told her he thought he should leave. And she had studied him with a very guarded look as he explained. But once she realized what he was saying, she had begun to grin. When he'd looked at her curiously, it took her a moment to explain.

"It's just funny. You're going to try and sneak back into the house I used to try and sneak out of."

He had had to admit she had a point. "I just don't want them mad at me."

Her mouth quirked upward once more. "Well, since Gram's the one who told me I would be a fool to turn you down, I wouldn't worry about it too much."

Rand would never forget standing there half-naked, gaping at her, boggled by her words. "Your grandmother…she what?"

And that's when she had started to laugh, a lovely sound that sent a tickle up his spine and made him want nothing more than to climb right back into bed with her and start all over again.

He made it back to his room just after one, without waking the Crawfords. Or at least if he had, they'd chosen not to confront him. Once safely inside, he took out the cell phone he'd turned off tonight and powered it back up. He was in bed and getting gloomy about how empty it felt when the phone chirped at him, announcing he had voice mail.

With a sigh he picked it up. He was relieved to find there was only one voice mail pending, but unhappy when it turned out to be a laconic message from St. John telling him to call. It was from three hours ago, so for a moment he considered waiting until morning. But only for a moment; everybody on the Redstone security team knew St. John never seemed to sleep. He made the call.

"About time," the rough, gravelly voice said without preamble.

"Even Josh takes Sunday night off," Rand said mildly.

St. John made a sound that could have been assent or simply a grunt. "Tuesday," he said.

Rand's brows furrowed. "Tues— The next shipment?"

"Yes."

"Thanks."

St. John disconnected without further comment. Rand shook his head. Four words, he thought. That was taking terse to new heights. He was even worse than Draven. Not that it was surprising. On the occasions when he'd encountered the man, Rand had thought him the most buttoned-up man he'd ever met.

Tuesday, he thought. That meant the shipment would be loaded tomorrow night. He'd better get to sleep tonight, since he clearly wouldn't be getting any tomorrow.

Kate felt a pang of doubt and isolation when she awoke alone, but was determined not to let it take hold. She'd gone into this with her eyes open. And she couldn't deny there was a lot to be said for taking a younger man as a lover.

Her body clenched at the flood of memories her thoughts brought on. Yes, there was a lot to be said, all right. As long as she remembered the affair was doomed from the start. She would simply keep her heart safely locked away, and she'd be all right.

Determinedly she tried to push thoughts of Rand out of her mind. It was difficult, because her body was reminding her of him at every turn. It wasn't just the unaccustomed tenderness in some delicate areas, or even the faint marks of passion that she found on her skin when she prepared for her shower. It was that her body seemed to be humming, everything seemed more vivid, even her breathing seemed different, the air cleaner and fresher.

Think about work, she ordered herself.

She was a quite a bit later getting up than she usually was, and she would be late going in, but her plans for the night made it better that she'd slept in. For a moment Rand crept back into her thoughts as she wondered if he might call or come by, wanting to go out again. She'd have to tell him she had to work, if he did. That made her mouth twist as she told herself not to expect anything from him.

When she got to the office her phone was ringing. She picked it up as she tossed her purse into a desk drawer.

"Kate Crawford."

"Hello, dear," her grandmother said. "I called earlier but got that voice-mail thing."

"Hi, Gram," she said as she tugged off her jacket.

"How was your evening with Rand?"

Leave it to Gram to cut right to the chase. Glad she wasn't having this conversation face-to-face, she managed to say, "Fine. We had a nice dinner."

"He got in rather late. Tried to sneak in, but that one step still creaks."

I should have warned him about that, Kate thought, remembering all times she'd forgotten about that step and betrayed herself. "Good thing he's a big boy and doesn't have to worry about curfew."

"Well, you tell him not to worry about waking us up anymore," her grandmother said in a tone that made clear she suspected her granddaughter had more than a little to do with their boarder's late return. Kate thought it best to just dodge the matter altogether. She hadn't quite worked her mind around how she was going to integrate this new aspect of her life, and until she did, the less she said—or admitted to—the better.

She managed to distract her grandmother and escape further inquisition. Then she turned her attention to the things that had to be done today. And as had become an unpleasant but necessary part of her routine, she checked her desk and her computer for any sign either had been used or tampered with since she was last here. Finding no signs on either, she went to work.

She had the routine stuff out of the way by late afternoon, and she sat back in her chair for a moment. Everything else could wait, and there was no putting it off any longer. The next shipment had to be boxed and loaded, and she'd given orders they weren't to start until she was there to observe every step.

When she arrived at the stockroom, they were waiting for her. There was an undeniable tension in the room; everyone here knew what was going on. Brian, the security guard, looked particularly nervous; Kate was sure he was afraid he'd be losing his job if they didn't resolve these thefts soon. She could relate to his worry; she wasn't sure she wouldn't lose hers, either.

Then she personally walked with the shipment to the loading dock. She watched as the boxes were loaded into the delivery van, and the back and side doors were locked. She drove it herself over to the mechanic's shop, and put the keys in the night mechanic's lockbox and secured it.

Knowing she'd done all she could for the moment, she went back to her office. She adjusted the miniblinds so that no one could see in, then opened the sliding closet door to the right of her desk, revealing the two new video monitors that had been installed over the weekend. One was trained on the exit gate, the other on the mechanic's shop itself. They both appeared to be working perfectly. She could see Brian standing just inside the shop door, his gaze trained steadily on the loaded truck.

They had worked this out ahead of time, and she knew

the young man would do his job diligently until she relieved him. She quickly finished the last details for the
day, then closed and locked her office. She announced to
all that she was leaving, putting the next phase of her plan
into action.

She drove home, quickly put together something to eat
and a snack for later, then curled up on her living room sofa
for a nap. The hoped-for sleep didn't come.

So much for trying to rest out here, she thought.

She'd decided it would be better out here than in the
bedroom where memories of last night would intrude. But
she was beginning to realize those memories weren't going
to be easily fought off, nor was the longing she couldn't
quite tamp down. She'd gone into this thinking as long as
she stayed casual about it, she'd be all right. She clearly
hadn't spent enough time considering if she'd be able to
accomplish that casualness.

When at last she dozed, she might as well have laid
down in the bed that still held his scent, because images of
him, naked and golden, still populated her restless dreams.

She awoke to the sound of the kitchen timer she'd set.
Twilight was already fading; it would be dark soon. She
got up, slipped her sheepskin boots back on, went to the
kitchen and splashed some cold water on her face to clear
her groggy head.

"Probably would have been better off just staying
awake," she muttered to herself.

She dried off, took the grocery bag she'd tucked some
cheese and crackers and a couple of caffeine laden sodas
into out of the fridge, then went to get her long, heavy coat,
in case she got stuck outside somewhere.

She carried it all out to her car. Once she was loaded up,
she started the car and headed down her long driveway

through the trees. She turned onto a side street about a hundred feet before the Redstone driveway, drove to the end where there was a gravel driveway that led to an empty building lot. She turned the car around, and backed up off the road, so she was parked heading back toward the street. She got out, gathered her things and locked the door.

And then she set off through the trees to try and catch a thief.

Chapter 17

Rand got out of his car and stood for a moment, gauging the chill in the air. He weighed the temperature against how long he was likely to be out in it, and then reached in for his heavy jacket. He pulled it on, then grabbed his large cup of coffee, thinking he might be wishing for a thermos of the stuff before the night was over. And this time, he took out his .38 and clipped the holster at the small of his book.

He found his way to his observation spot easily even in the dark now. He settled in with the replacement night-vision binoculars he'd had shipped to him from the security team locker at the airport near Redstone headquarters. It wasn't dark, so he didn't turn them on yet.

He looked into the complex below. There were a handful of cars parked in the lot. He recognized them as belonging to the people who worked the night shift. Everyone who was there was inside, as far as he could tell. Not that he could blame them, when it was this cold out.

You've gotten soft, he chided himself. *Too much time spent in sunny California.*

He waited, thinking that this was the last time he was going to do this. If there was another theft and he didn't find or see anything, then this method obviously wasn't going to work. He'd have to try another approach. Of course, if it did work, then he'd be done here. As far as his job was concerned, anyway.

Kate was a different matter.

A sudden burst of heat warmed him against the cold. It happened every time he thought about last night, thought about how amazing it had been. He'd known it would be good between them, but he'd never imagined just how good.

He still wondered why she'd changed her mind. She'd apparently gotten over her mistrust of him about her grandparents. But she'd still seemed pretty hung up on the age difference between them, although it was something he hadn't even thought about last night.

Whatever it was, he certainly wasn't going to question his good fortune. If she'd managed to put her reservations out of her mind, or better yet, her feelings had overcome them, then he was not about to remind her of them. He didn't want anything to get in the way of what they had found together.

A shiver rippled through him that had nothing to do with the cold and everything to do with memories of the hours spent in Kate's bed. His body clenched at the images that flashed through his mind. He already resented spending tonight freezing up here on this hillside when he could have been back in her warm, cozy house, learning more about her delicious responsiveness.

And, he realized, learning about her. It surprised him a little, how much he wanted to know about her. Not just her taste in things, food, movies, books, but how she felt and thought about…well, about everything.

He snapped out of his reverie when he realized full darkness had descended. He reached for the night-vision binoculars, turned them on, and began to scan the plant below him.

He'd not even finished his first scan of the area when a rather furtive movement caught his eye. He moved the binoculars back to where he'd seen the motion. After a couple of seconds he spotted what he'd seen; a slim human figure moving toward the main building, keeping close to the wall, staying in the shadows.

He worked the focus ring to sharpen the image. The green tint made it look odd, but he knew that courtesy of some speeding electrons he was seeing a lot more than he would with the naked eye. And since this was the first suspicious thing he'd seen, he knew it was significant. Whoever it was, they clearly didn't want to be seen, and that alone made them suspect one just now.

The figure paused, then looked around. He saw the face.

His gut knotted in instant, intense protest. He didn't want to believe it. Felt faintly nauseous at the thought that he might have to believe it. Because there was no denying what the binoculars were showing him.

It was Kate.

With only her small desk lamp and the glow of her computer screen for light, Kate worked on the various projects she'd set aside to do tonight. She had turned her chair to face the closet, where the two video monitors were turned on and registering absolutely nothing unexpected. The delivery truck she had parked and locked herself sat exactly where she had left it, just outside the shop door. The only thing that had happened at all was the arrival of the night mechanic a half an hour ago. The man had parked his own white van beside the delivery truck, and then got out and walked toward the shop. The main lights inside had gone on shortly after that, but so far nothing else was happening.

She glanced again at the two screens. In the movies or television, there was always one of the bad guys who managed to tamper with the feed or substitute a tape of nothing happening to hide the criminal activity. But in this case, no one but she and Brian even knew the cameras were there, so there was little chance they'd be interfered with. Still, she kept her attention firmly divided and watched regularly for long periods.

Finally, the next time she glanced up she saw the night mechanic step into the pool of light from the floodlight above the shop. She saw he had retrieved the keys she'd locked away. When he unlocked the delivery truck's driver's door, she set down the reports she'd been working on and focused completely on the video monitor.

The mechanic reached into the cab of the truck and bent slightly. She saw the hood move, and realized he had pulled the inside release latch. He backed out of the cab, straightened the baseball cap he'd apparently bumped during the maneuver, and walked around to the front of the truck. He lifted the hood the rest of the way, and bent over to peer into the engine compartment.

Kate recognized the familiar motions of checking oil and the other fluids. The man stepped out of the light, then back in as he went about his business, twice walking toward his van, vanishing, then returning with a tool. The brim of the cap shadowed his face, but she could see his actions clearly.

Then Kate watched as he got down on the ground and scooted under the truck. They had a rack in the shop, she knew, but guessed for whatever quick once-over he was doing he'd decided it wasn't worth it. She watched for several minutes while he did whatever he was doing underneath. She was starting to wonder if he'd found something wrong when he finally reappeared. He pulled a rag out of the back pocket of his Redstone overalls and wiped his hands off. He walked back to the front and lowered the hood. She saw him put some weight onto it to be sure it latched.

She watched as he walked around to the back of the truck, which was in full view of the camera. She leaned forward, thinking that if anything was going to happen, it would be now. But all he did was reach up and tug on the door handle, as if making certain it was still locked. It didn't give, and he patted the back door.

She watched as he disappeared between the two vehicles. A minute or two later, she saw his van pull away. Her forehead creased when he drove out of the yard and headed for the exit; she didn't think he was supposed to be off until midnight.

She switched her gaze to the exit camera, and just about when she expected it she saw the van pull through the gate. She'd have to ask the shop manager in the morning about the night guy's hours. Maybe he'd made arrangements to leave early.

For a long time she sat there watching the truck, wondering if and when the thief would show up. Eventually she went back to her other tasks, but still kept an eye closely on the monitors. After another two hours, even the extra caffeine she'd consumed wasn't enough, and she began to yawn.

Finally dawn arrived. She walked to the window, opened

the blinds and watched the sky grow lighter, too tired to control her tumbling thoughts any longer. They careened back and forth between her problems here and her fledgling relationship with Rand. She wasn't sure where either was headed, and she didn't like the feeling.

At last she saw the truck driver's car pull in. She filed away the things she'd been working on, then shut down and secured her computer. She slipped on her coat, got her purse out of the drawer and headed outside.

"Good morning, Jim," she said as she neared the van.

The man spun around, as if she'd startled him. "Oh, Ms. Crawford. You're here early." He grimaced. "Guess you've got reason."

"Yes," she said. "I'd like to look in the back, if you don't mind."

"No problem," he said, and walked to the back of the truck.

"The keys were in the lockbox?" she asked.

"Yes ma'am," he said. "Right where they were supposed to be."

She nodded as he unlocked the door. She looked in and saw the cartons neatly stacked. She did a quick count and came up with the correct number. With a sigh, she watched as Jim closed and relocked the door.

"I'd say I'll do my best, but I have been all along," Jim said.

Kate reached out and patted his arm. "I know you have, Jim. We just have to hope this time will be different."

She watched him drive off. Then she headed for her own car, wondering if the thief had been scared off, or simply decided not to go for this shipment. Could he have found out about the cameras? They were well hidden, and had been installed late Sunday night, but it might be possible someone had seen it.

Which would prove that someone had to be on the inside, that Redstone indeed had a spy, or the actual thief, under their own roof.

Wearily she walked to her car and started home.

Rand put the night-vision binoculars back into the case with exaggerated care. Not that they weren't expensive and didn't need to be handled carefully, but he concentrated on the task as if they were made of spun sugar.

Kate.

Damn it, Kate….

He tried to rein himself in. There was no denying or changing what he'd seen. On the night before a shipment, she had shown up after dark, sneaking in, staying in the shadows, obviously worried about someone seeing her.

But…he also knew she'd had the surveillance cameras installed. That had been St. John's message.

He couldn't think about it now. He had a job to do. He went down the hill at a run, and cleared the fallen log between him and his car in a leap. In less than a minute he was on the road, and in less than two had the delivery truck in sight. He knew where they were going, he had the delivery schedule, but he wanted to keep the vehicle in sight, to see what, if anything, happened en route.

Nothing did.

He had the truck in view all the way to Tacoma, where the first boxes were due to be dropped off at a medical supply company. He quickly picked his spot across the street, and parked to watch the delivery.

Rand knew the instant the man in the white coat picked up the first box. He didn't have to see them open the box. There was no mistaking his puzzled look and the awkward movement of a man picking up a box he'd expected to weigh something but didn't.

They did open it, and as he expected by then, found it empty. They opened the rest of the boxes, with the same results. And he didn't need to be a lip reader to grasp the driver's profanity laced reaction.

Rand didn't like how this was adding up. They'd been hit again. And it hadn't happened after the truck had left Redstone, nor did he believe the driver was involved; the man's fury was palpable even from here. Which meant the thefts had to have happened while the shipment was still at Redstone. Which also meant someone on the inside was involved.

And the only person he'd seen doing anything at all suspicious was Kate.

He couldn't believe it.

You don't want to believe it, was his rational mind's quick response.

He wasn't sure which was the truth. Maybe both.

He couldn't stand this. He had to know. Had to know before he got in any deeper than he already was. He pulled back out into the midday traffic and headed back north. He wasn't sure exactly what he was going to do, only that he had to find out once and for all if Kate was the thief. Only then could he go on with getting his job done. If she wasn't, then he could focus elsewhere with out this powerful distraction. If she was…

If she was, he didn't know what he'd do. Rand groaned inwardly as he realized he was already in way too deep to escape unscathed.

Chapter 18

He was about to turn into Kate's driveway when his cell rang. A glance at the ID readout showed him the call was from Redstone headquarters. He pulled over and flipped the phone open.

"Singleton."

"Hi, sweetie."

He smiled at the sound of Sam's voice. "Hey, lady."

"Any news?"

"All bad, I'm afraid."

"Got hit again?"

"And not after the shipment left."

"Ouch," Sam said, instantly realizing what his words meant. "Any idea who's on the inside?"

"There's…a possibility or two." Even to Sam, one of his closest friends and his frequent partner, he couldn't bring himself to mention Kate in that context.

"Well, I've got some info for you on one of your possibles. St. John handed it off to me before he left."

"Left? For where?"

"Who knows? You know how he is."

He did. Anybody who worked at Redstone for long did. There was little that went on that St. John didn't know, and Josh himself often said that if anything happened to him, St. John could take over in a heartbeat and run it all. While everybody agreed the man was uncannily omnipresent, none of them would ever wish him in Josh's place, because he lacked the one thing Josh had in abundance—the ability to deal with the human factor. St. John tended to expect everyone to be like he himself—cool, controlled and unemotional in all circumstances.

There had been, for a while, a contest at headquarters to see if anyone could make the man laugh. No one had ever won the pot. That hadn't really surprised anyone, but they'd all been startled when St. John calmly claimed the prize, saying since they'd all lost, he must have won. No one knew how he'd found out, and it had only added to his reputation of knowing everything that went on at Redstone.

"What he left me," Sam said, "is the financial report on Katherine Crawford you asked for."

Rand's jaw tightened. "And?"

"It's quite something."

Damn. He'd hoped, when he hadn't heard back right away, that there had simply been nothing to find. "Go ahead," he said, even though he knew he wasn't going to like what he was about to hear.

"She's in a hole, all right. Took some digging to find out why. It's pretty sad."

"Sad?" He was certain it wasn't drugs, or booze. Was she a closet compulsive gambler?

"Apparently she went deep in debt, sold her house, and robbed her 401K, all for the same reason. Her little girl."

Rand blinked. "What?"

"That's why this took so long. Getting medical info is tricky. Even Redstone research was only able to get the basics. Apparently the baby was born with multiple, life-threatening health problems. By the time she was two, she was in the hospital more than out."

"And Kate spent everything trying to save her."

"Yes." If Sam noticed his use of the nickname, she didn't comment on it. But then, Sam had always been the soul of discretion.

"What about her husband?" he asked, wondering why the man hadn't even been mentioned.

"Oh, now there's a real man." Sam's tone was unusually sour. "According to this, he bailed the minute he found out the baby wasn't perfect, that they were looking at long-term problems. Left her holding the bag, the baby and the bills."

When the going got tough, he got going—to a divorce lawyer, Kate had told him.

"Bastard," Rand said. No wonder Sam was angry; that kind of thing was a hot button for her. Her little brother had some long-term problems of his own, and Sam had spent most of her adult life fighting for him.

"My sentiments exactly. No wonder the first thing she did after the child died was take her maiden name back." Then, as if giving in to curiosity, she asked, "What's she like?"

All the things he felt about Kate bubbled up and threatened to come pouring out. He bit them back, not even to Sam could he spill the truth about how much trouble he was in on this job. If he told her, he knew she'd feel compelled to come rescue him, and right now he wasn't sure he wanted to be rescued.

"She's exactly what you'd expect a woman who would do that for her child to be."

"But is she the thief?"

"I hope not." And that, he thought, was the understatement of all time.

"You all right, partner?"

No, he said silently. "I will be," he said aloud. "I just hope I don't have to destroy some people I like to resolve this."

"Good luck," Sam said softly.

He knew she meant it. After they'd disconnected he sat there for a few minutes. Maybe he should have talked to Sam. Who would better understand? She'd told him about how she'd fought her attraction to Ian, when he'd been her assignment.

And she'd lost that fight, he reminded himself. But she'd won, in the end. The biggest prize of all.

He needed to think. And make some decisions. With a sigh, he put the car back in gear. He went past Kate's driveway, past the turnoff to the Crawford's house, and kept on going. He wasn't sure where he was going. But sooner or later in this land of beautiful vistas, he'd find one to park and stare at, while he tried to make sense out of the tangle he was in.

When the phone rang, Kate was so soundly asleep that she sat up completely disoriented. It was a gray day, dark enough that for a moment she thought it was either dawn or twilight. By the second ring she had glanced at the clock, and had managed to remember it was instead midmorning.

Moments later, as she hung up, she was wide-awake. Wide-awake, and furious. This time they'd done it literally right under her nose.

She leaped to her feet and dressed hurriedly. She

couldn't remember the last time she'd been so angry. Even when Dan had walked out, she'd been so consumed with worry about her child that she'd had little emotion to spare for her deserter husband.

She arrived at her office with her anger still running high. Her greetings were uncharacteristically terse; she was in no mood to be cheerful, and she couldn't help wondering which of them was the traitor. The only other option was Jim, the driver, and she just didn't believe it.

Of course, she didn't want to believe it of anyone.

She spent the rest of the morning watching the hours of video from last night, never taking her eyes off the screen without pausing the tape. Even on fast forward, her already tired eyes were gritty by the time she reached the halfway point. And she saw nothing she hadn't already seen.

Watching it reminded her, however, and she picked up the phone and called the shop manager. He told her the night mechanic sometimes went home for his lunch break. That explained, she went back to work.

She spent the afternoon going through every person on the staff here, making a list of reasons why they could or could not be the culprit. When she was done she threw her pen down on her desk in disgust. She hated having to think this way about people she worked with and liked. Hated having to think in such negative ways about them, trying to remember anything they'd ever said or done that might hint at trouble. She was no good at it, never had been.

She thought she'd left this kind of thinking behind, in the city, in the corporate world she'd escaped. She'd even been hesitant to take the job with Redstone, for fear of finding more of the same. But Redstone was a different beast altogether, Redstone was like a family, and Redstone people looked out for each other.

She stood up and began to pace, trying to think. She'd been through this so many times she didn't see how she could think of anything new, but she was determined. She'd always worked well under pressure, under a deadline. So she'd just give herself one.

"I'm not leaving this office until I have a plan," she said out loud, and hearing the words solidified her resolve.

She walked over to the window, to look down at this place that had restored her joy in doing productive work. She went through it once more in her mind, every step she'd taken yesterday and last night, trying to see where she'd missed something. From the packing of the boxes to the loading, to the night spent with the truck's doors secured and undisturbed, to the recheck in the morning and Jim's departure. She couldn't see where she'd missed anything as blatant as the theft of the entire shipment.

But as she stared toward the loading dock, the germ of an idea glimmered in her mind. She turned her head to look at the shop area. She walked out of her office and headed across the courtyard.

"You look tired," Rand said. Of course, he knew she was, and he knew why, but it seemed like he should say something anyway.

She sipped at the last of the glass of lemonade she'd ordered with her fish and chips. "I am. I went in to work last night."

He lifted a brow at her across the restaurant table. "Odd. I drove by there and didn't see your car."

She gave him a startled look. Did it also hold guilt? He couldn't tell. And again he wondered what she would do when she, as she inevitably would, learned the truth about who he was and why he was here.

"I...I parked a ways away. To walk. For the exercise."

She was not a practiced liar. Or she was so practiced she knew how to make it look that way. "At night?" he asked mildly.

"This isn't the big city," she said. "It's quite safe here."

"Safer," he agreed. "But I'm sure even Summer Harbor has the occasional crime. You know, vandalism, a theft now and then."

She didn't look at him this time. He wondered if she was afraid of what he might read in her expression.

"Of course we do. It only looks like Eden."

Something in her voice made his stomach knot. He couldn't do this. Not to her. He couldn't keep poking at her, to see if she'd let anything slip.

"That wasn't a criticism, Kate. I know you love this place. And I can see why."

She smiled then, and his gut relaxed. And even as it happened, he was ruefully aware he'd never been so befuddled before. Just when he'd decided she was, regretfully, the most likely suspect, something like what Sam had relayed came up, and he was convinced she couldn't be all over again. No matter that she was the one with the best opportunity, a motive and the brains to pull this off over and over again, it just didn't fit with who she was.

Or who he thought she was.

He couldn't deny that he was too involved to be objective. Nor could he deny what it was going to do to him if he was wrong. It was a dilemma that had no solution at the moment, and wouldn't until he unraveled this case.

But for now, he chose to believe she was the woman who loved her grandparents enough to change her life to care for them, just as she had loved her child enough to sell everything she owned and mortgage her future to give her a chance.

"I was going to suggest a movie or something, but I think I'd better just get you home so you can get some sleep."

"I...thank you."

She was very quiet as they drove back to her house. Except to give him directions at an intersection marked by nothing more than a dead tree and a broken fence, she barely spoke until they were standing on her front porch.

"Thank you," she said again.

"My pleasure."

He leaned down to her. He meant only to give her a good-night kiss, simple and quick. But the moment his mouth touched her lips, that heat that flared so quickly scorched all his good intentions.

He barely managed to pull away before he was completely out of control. When he saw an echoing heat reflected in Kate's eyes, he nearly lost his resolve.

"You want to come in...for that 'or something'?"

The rich, husky note that had come into her voice completed the job of crumbling his determination to go away and let her rest.

"Are you sure you're not too tired?"

"I was," she said, "until you kissed me."

And with that simple declaration Rand was lost. He'd never before felt like those few words made him feel. He didn't know if it was the straightforwardness of them, or simply that it was Kate saying them. He didn't care. He only knew that for her he would put his job, his common sense, and everything else on hold. He already had.

But he hadn't forgotten how tired she was, although he tried not to think about the reason why.

"Let me," he said softly as she fumbled with her coat. And she did.

He said it again when they were in her bedroom, and again she let him. He undressed her carefully, gently, telling himself that if she fell asleep he would let her be. But instead she sat down on the edge of the bed, watching him as he pulled off his own clothes.

"You're as beautiful as I remember," she whispered, and his belly tightened.

"I think that's my line," he said. "Because you are, Katy. You are."

She held her arms up to him then, and he went down to her like wax.

"Let me," he said a third time. "You just relax, and let me take care of you. Just for tonight, Kate, let someone else do the worrying."

She lay back then, looked at him for a long, silent moment. Then she nodded. He began slowly, tenderly tracing every curve and hollow, stroking and petting and until she began to move restlessly beneath his touch. He kept on, until there wasn't a part of her he hadn't explored.

Then he started all over again with his mouth, following the same paths, savoring the hot silk of her skin and the luscious, female softness. He kissed, tasted, licked and suckled until she was moaning, a low, rough sound that made his already aroused flesh ache.

When at last he slid into her, she was hot, slick and ready, and she cried out his name in welcome. He began to move, trying to concentrate on her, but it was nearly impossible when she began to move with him, meeting his every thrust, rousing him to a fever pitch only heightened by the sound and sensation of their bodies joining.

He bit his lip, trying to hold back, desperate not to lose control. And then she cried out, and he felt her body begin to clench around him as her fingers dug into his hips as if she were trying to pull him inside her. He felt the undeniable urge to help her, and ground his hips harder against her. Her name burst from him as his body convulsed and wave after wave of hot, pulsing sensation poured through him.

He collapsed on top of her, gasping, the world spinning around him as if there truly wasn't enough air in the room. He felt tiny echoes of pleasure ripple through him in response to the caress of her flesh around him.

He tried to think of something to say, something profound, something she would remember when she finally learned who he really was and why he was in Summer Harbor. She would be, he had little doubt, furious at him for deceiving her. He had to find a way to somehow convince her that no matter the circumstances, this was real and precious and good.

Before he could find the words to say anything at all, she had surrendered to sleep. And so he stayed silent, holding her close, realizing for the first time just how much he had to lose if this all went sour on him.

He lay awake for a long time.

Kate's plan was coming together, and it made her feel energized.

Or maybe, she thought with an inward smile, it was as much thanks to Rand as anything else. He'd kept her so occupied this past week that she hadn't had time to stress about what was going on at work. And when she did go to the office, she was, after a night with Rand, refreshed and more than ready to tackle anything.

Even you.

Her thought was directed at that faceless, unknown betrayer she was more determined than ever to discover.

Everything was in place. Tonight was the night. She'd

already told Rand she had to work late tonight. She'd asked him to drop her off, so that her car wouldn't be there for anyone to track her comings and goings. He'd been puzzled, but had accepted her hurried "I'll explain later."

She had sent the altered schedule to the shipping department three days ago, with word that they were speeding production to make up for the lost shipments. Plenty of warning for the thief. She had taken only Brian into her confidence, and he was helping her now. Between them they sealed up the boxes, with Kate putting a barely noticeable mark in the same place on each taped seam so she could later tell if they'd been opened and retaped.

When they were done she stepped back to look. The boxes looked exactly like all the other shipments. And from here on, that's how they would be handled. The only difference was that the next shipment hadn't been scheduled to go for two more weeks.

Well that, and the fact that these boxes were full of carefully weighed Redstone logo pens instead of the precious insulin pumps.

And she alone knew that. Even Brian thought the boxes were full of what was stated on the manifest; she'd only brought him in after she'd packed the boxes by hand herself.

She thanked him for his help, and sent him on his way. She waited for the loading crew, because she wanted this to seem the same as before. She watched as they loaded the shipment into the truck, none of them apparently noticing anything unusual about the boxes they were hefting.

She again took over the truck, and moved it to the shop. She hung the keys in the mechanic's lockbox as always.

Only this time, she had a duplicate of the shop's key in her pocket.

* * *

This was, perhaps, not the greatest idea she'd ever had.

Kate was willing to admit that. In fact, she had little choice, considering how cold she was. But she couldn't think of anything else to do, and she desperately needed to feel as if she were doing something.

She sat huddled in a corner, wishing yet again that she'd brought something to sit on. The cold from the concrete beneath her was seeping through even her heavy coat.

At least her feet were warm, thanks to her sheepskin boots. That helped. That, and being mostly out of the wind that had kicked up after sundown.

A loud thud made her jump, and she barely managed to hold back a startled exclamation. Her head snapped around to look in the direction of the sound, and she saw a large branch that had obviously broken from a tree and hit the metal side of the shop building.

She let out a sigh and returned to her vigil. This wind was making it very hard for her to distinguish natural noises from anything that might be human-caused. Of course, that was why she was out here, huddled between the Dumpster and the wall of the shop. She'd decided that just seeing, as on the video surveillance monitors, wasn't enough. She wanted to hear as well. So she'd come back again after dark, checked the load and found the boxes undisturbed, including her marks, and then settled down to wait it out.

And in the end, she didn't hear a thing. But she saw the man, just a fleeting glimpse as he darted from the shadows of the far side of the shop over to the truck. On the side, she noted, away from the camera.

Her heart began to race as she realized that the way he'd done it, there was every chance the video cameras wouldn't have picked him up, or it would have been only a split second that would have been easy to overlook. And she could easily have missed it when she was fast forwarding through the tapes. She leaned forward, holding her breath as she strained to see and hear.

Whoever it was, they were obviously very good. She saw nothing, heard nothing. Seconds ticked by, and she knew she had to do something, before the thief got away. This was as close as she'd gotten and she might never get a better chance. She might never get another chance at all.

She crept out of her hiding place, her cell phone with the police number ready to be dialed in one hand, a can of pepper spray in the other. She tried to keep the bulk of the van between her and the man. Slowly, barely daring to breathe, she crept closer. She knew about where she'd last seen him, and if she could—

An arm came around her from behind. It tightened, choking off her scream. She dropped the pepper spray. Barely hung onto her phone.

She'd never heard a thing.

"Kate?"

She went very still. The pressure on her throat eased. She tried to process the information that whispered hiss of her name gave her. Tried to make sense of it. Tried to make it something other than what she knew it was.

It was Rand.

Chapter 19

"What the *hell* do you think you're doing?"

He'd released her from his choke hold, but spun her around to face him. He winced when her hand went up to her throat and rubbed at it as she stared at him, her eyes wide with shock.

"That—" Her voice cracked, making him feel even worse. "That should be my question, don't you think?"

"Kate," he began, instinctively reaching for her. She backed up a step, away from him. Hastily, as if she were afraid of him. A wave of nausea swept him at the thought.

She lifted her other hand, and he realized she had her cell phone. She kept watching him as she put it to her ear.

"I called earlier, and now I need a deputy here. I've…caught the thief."

The cops. She was calling the sheriff. Rand sighed inwardly. "Kate, stop."

"Yes, I have him here right now." She gave Rand a startled look. "No, I don't believe he's armed."

There was no hope for it. He reached into his back pocket. Kate backed up even farther, hastily. He realized she was thinking he might actually have a weapon, and turned sideways so she could see he was only pulling out his wallet. Her brow furrowed, but she kept talking to the dispatcher on the phone.

He flipped open his wallet to his Redstone ID, and held it in front of her. At first she ignored it, but finally he saw her focus on the card with his photograph. In the middle of confirming the address, her voice trailed off. Her gaze shot to his face.

"Ma'am? Ma'am?"

Rand could hear the dispatcher's voice as he called out to Kate, clearly worrying that something had happened.

"I'm sorry. Never mind," Kate said into the phone in a tiny voice he'd never heard from her before.

"Never mind?"

Kate seemed to pull herself together, and when she spoke this time, her voice was steadier. "I am sorry. Cancel the call, please. It appears to be a case of…mistaken identity."

He knew he wasn't mistaking the undertone in her voice, he just couldn't decide if it was anger, bitterness or both. She answered a couple more questions from the dispatcher. Then she closed her phone. She slipped it into her coat pocket.

"Are you crazy?" The words burst from him. "What if I had been the thief, and had a gun?"

"I had pepper spray ready."

She looked around on the ground, and he realized that must have been what he'd heard drop when he'd grabbed her.

"Pepper spray's useless against a bullet. Damn it, you could have been hurt! Or worse," he ended grimly.

She crossed her arms in front of her in an unambiguous display of self-protective body language.

"I wasn't."

"But you could have been."

She let out an audible breath. "All right, but I didn't think of that."

"Were you thinking at all?"

"Yes," she snapped. "If I hadn't been, I would have gone with my first idea, which was waiting inside the truck."

Dear God, he thought, his guts twisting at the possibilities of that hammered his suddenly overactive imagination.

"Damn," he muttered.

"Well, I didn't do it. And besides, I called the sheriff's office ahead of time, told them if they got another call from me I'd need them here in a hurry, whether I could say anything to them or not."

Well, that was smart enough, he thought. Calmer now, he let it go and tried again. "Kate, listen."

"Oh, I'm listening. To the voice in my head saying that I've never been a bigger fool."

"You're not a fool."

"Oh? Then why did it never occur to me that Redstone would send someone?"

"Because you don't think like that," he said. "You handle your own problems."

And suddenly, belatedly he realized that he had all the proof he needed that Kate was not now and had never been involved in the thefts. Relief flooded him, and he couldn't help smiling.

Kate stiffened. "Funny, is it?"

"No, it's not, it's just that—"

"Maybe I just didn't realize our little problem would draw the elite. I know the reputation of the Redstone security team. Anybody who works here for long does. Why would I think they would turn up here in little Summer Harbor?"

"You had no way of knowing."

"Sure."

He glanced around. Time was passing, and he still had a job to do. This was going to have to wait.

"Look, I came here tonight to do something, and I need to get it done. And get out of here, in case our boy shows up early. Then we can talk all you want."

"Came to do what?"

She had the right to know, he supposed, all things considered. He reached into his inside jacket pocket and pulled out what had arrived from Redstone just yesterday.

"It's a tracking device," he said, showing her the small receiver and the even smaller transmitter. "GPS based and motion activated. It'll go off the minute this load changes geographic coordinates. I need to slip it into one of the boxes."

She hesitated only an instant and then nodded, and he realized just how well he'd come to know her by the way he could tell she'd decided to set her own feelings aside for the moment for the sake of catching the thief.

She unlocked the door for him, saving him the trouble of picking the lock. Quickly he placed the transmitter in one of the top boxes.

"Wouldn't it be better in one of the bottom ones? Maybe delay it being found?"

He looked over his shoulder at her. "Good idea. But think about how the thief will likely go about transferring the boxes."

She saw it immediately. "He'll take the top ones first, so they'll become the bottom."

"Exactly."

She shook her head. "You're right. I don't think that way."

"Thank goodness," he said as he activated the transmitter and checked to make sure the receiver was reading it. "I have enough trouble with the dumb crooks without having smart ones in the woodwork."

The compliment had been intentional, but he could see by her expression when he hopped out of the back of the truck that she wasn't ready to forgive him. Yet, he thought, trying to be optimistic.

"We're set," he said.

"Now what?"

He considered that for a moment. "We go to my car and turn on the heater while we wait."

"Now there's an offer I can't refuse," she muttered.

No, she wasn't anywhere near ready, he thought.

She gave him a sideways look as he led the way past the building that housed her office, and up the hill behind it. "Can you make it?"

"I climbed Rainier once," she said, "so I guess I can manage this."

Well, well, she was just full of surprises. And she proved the truth of what she'd said by easily keeping pace with him until they were over the rise and headed down to where his car was parked.

By the time they had moved to where he got a clear signal from the transmitter, the car was comfortably warm. Kate turned sideways in her seat to look at him. Her mouth twisted.

"Pretty good, Singleton. You had me so fooled I called the cops on our own security."

He winced again at her use of his last name. He'd known she'd be mad, but he hadn't expected it to sting this much. "At least you called the cops," he said.

"What?"

"If you hadn't, you might still be on the suspect list."

She stared at him. "Me?" Then her expression changed, became thoughtful. "Of course. Who would have a better chance than I to pull this off?"

"Yes. You had knowledge, opportunity and motive."

She eyed him steadily. "The motive being what? Money, I suppose?"

He nodded. "What you didn't have was the mindset to resort to stealing."

"My, I appreciate your faith in me," she said dryly.

She had a right to the sarcasm, he told himself. But he tried to explain anyway. "Kate, I couldn't tell you. Not until I was sure you weren't involved."

"I can understand that," she said, surprising him.

He let out a relieved breath. But her next words made him suck it back in again.

"So, that's why the charm? The persistence? The—"

"Kate, no!" He'd been afraid of this. "I tried to stay away, damn it. I knew I shouldn't get involved with you, not on a case."

"You mean while I was a suspect, don't you?"

"That, too," he admitted. "But I couldn't stay away. I kept telling myself it was crazy, but I couldn't back off. Every time something would happen that would make me suspect you, I couldn't make myself believe it."

"Something would happen?"

He nodded. "Like you going out on the nights of the thefts. Or being so edgy and jumpy on those days. Like you were afraid of being caught."

Kate drew back slightly. "Just how closely have you been watching me? And for how long?"

"Since I arrived," he said.

She grimaced. "So that's why you took the room at my grandparents'. You are using them."

"Not in the way you mean," he said. "I needed a place to stay. That it was their place was just good luck. I'd already decided to check into the room before I found out who they were."

"I see." She looked doubtful.

A desperate feeling roiled inside him. He put every bit of the turmoil he'd been feeling into his voice when he went on, "I couldn't be honest with you then, Kate. I hated deceiving you, but I had no choice."

Her expression shifted, and he thought he saw a tiny flicker of receptiveness. "You really mean that, don't you?"

"Yes."

"I would think you have to do a lot of lying in your job."

"Sometimes. I never like it, but when it's to good people I hate it." He took a breath before adding, "When it's to people I've come to…care about, I loathe it."

One corner of her mouth twitched. "You're just a regular Sir Galahad, aren't you?"

"Hardly. I'm just a guy doing a job."

"I don't know. You certainly look the part."

He blinked. Was she teasing him? He couldn't tell. He wasn't used to this floundering feeling, and he didn't much like it.

"You have every right to be angry," he began.

"But I'm not."

"You—" He stopped. "You're not?"

"No. I mean, even I can see that I was an obvious suspect, from your point of view. I feel pretty foolish, but I'm not angry."

"Don't feel foolish." His mouth quirked. "I'm pretty good at being undercover when I need to be."

"That I can believe. I'm just glad calling the police on you cleared me."

"You're being awfully reasonable about this." He was having a little trouble accepting her reaction. He'd expected a blowup at the least.

She smiled, but it was a smile more than touched by sadness. "Let's just say that in the larger scheme of things, something like this isn't…life-altering."

"Oh."

He didn't know what else to say, because he knew she meant she was comparing this to the loss of her child. And somehow telling her that he knew that about her, too, didn't seem to be the thing to do at this moment. And he wouldn't know what to say anyway; he couldn't even imagine the kind of pain that lost must have caused her. Didn't like even thinking about her hurting that badly.

She was looking at him curiously. "You'd rather I pitched a fit and screamed at you?"

"Maybe," he said. "I thought you'd be furious."

And he couldn't help wondering if the reason she wasn't angry was because she didn't care enough to be. Perverse, he thought. He didn't like the idea of her being hurt, but didn't like the idea he didn't have the power to hurt her, either.

The sudden beeping from the receiver on the front seat cut off his thoughts.

"It's party time," he muttered, and reached for the key to start the engine.

Chapter 20

Kate sat staring at the small device on the seat. It was about the size of a television remote control. A green light was blinking. It had started out slowly, but was now flashing more rapidly.

"What's that mean, when the light speeds up? The transmitter's getting closer?"

Rand nodded. "When it gets to within fifty feet, it stays lit. Within twenty-five and it'll beep."

"Clever."

"Very. So's the guy who invented it. In fact, he invented the sensor that made the insulin pump possible."

She gave him a sideways look. "You know him?"

"Yeah. He works for Redstone. He's also married to one of our team."

"The security team?" she asked.

"Yep. Samantha Beckett. Well, Gamble now. She's my usual partner, in fact."

"Oh."

So, his usual partner was a woman. She felt a small twinge. A married woman, she reminded herself. And he obviously had no problem with that.

"We kind of look alike, so sometimes we—"

He broke off, leaned forward, and moved his hand to the gear shift. Kate looked down and saw the light on the receiver was now a solid green. And by the time he'd put the car in drive, they saw headlights coming down the exit driveway. Moments later, the little box was quietly but definitely beeping.

"That's one of the shop vans," Kate said, brows furrowing as the familiar white vehicle exited the gate and turned right. "They told me the night mechanic goes home for his lunch break sometimes."

"Well," Rand said as he pulled out onto the road and headed after the van, "this time he's taking the transmitter with him. And likely the box it was in."

He didn't turn the headlights on, Kate noticed, but although he was clearly intent on his driving, he didn't seem to have any trouble. He kept well back from the van even without lights.

Kate stayed quiet, not wanting to disturb his concentration. In fact she was glad of the chance to think. And to wonder herself, as he had, why she wasn't angry. But what she'd said had been nothing less than the truth; she felt a bit foolish, but not angry, not beyond the first few minutes after his revelation.

In part, her lack of anger was because she was feeling that she really should have guessed. She should have realized that Redstone wouldn't let something like the theft of crucial medical equipment just slide. That ran counter to everything she had learned about Josh Redstone, and she should have known better. And her reaction, once she got past the shock—and the embarrassment of having slept with someone when she didn't even know who he really was—had been along the lines of "Well, of course."

The van made a quick turn to the right again, taking the corner fast enough to make the tires squeal. Rand slowed, glancing at her.

"Where's that go?"

"Up," she said. "It dead ends up on the bluff overlooking the cove."

"Any side roads?"

"Maybe two or three, but they're little more than driveways."

He negotiated the turn and started up the hill, still blacked out. "So they're likely to be heading somewhere on this road. What's there?"

"It's either residential or undeveloped, all the way to the top. Very quiet area."

"So they could be headed to a house. Or just to some open space."

"Either."

She thought for a moment, trying to remember the road in her mind. "As a kid I had a friend who lived about halfway up, so I know that first part fairly well. There's a big curve to the right just ahead, and then a really tight one to the left farther up."

He nodded. "And the rest?"

"I've only been up once or twice. When you get to the top, it's only gravel and has some spots that are really treacherous in the rain or with ice. Especially since it drops off to the sound about a hundred and fifty feet."

"Charming," he muttered.

"No guard rail, either," she added blithely.

Despite driving in the dark with no headlights, he gave her a quick sideways glance. "Trying to scare me?"

"Not at all. Surely it would take more than that to scare off one of Redstone's finest."

He laughed, but there was a rueful note in it. "Right now I'm not feeling much like the finest of anything. I should have had this solved long ago."

"So should I."

"It's not your job."

"It's my department. I'm responsible."

"You instigated new security procedures after the first theft. Good ones. That's all anyone expected."

"I'm sure that'll look good on my résumé when I'm looking for a new job."

There was a pause while he negotiated the big turn she'd warned him about. She caught a glimpse of the taillights of the van ahead, still moving.

"That," he said when the road had straightened out again, "is not Josh's style. He doesn't just chop off the manager's head. Besides, he's pleased with your work."

"He is?" She found it hard to believe that the man who ran an empire the size of Redstone paid any attention at all to tiny cogs like her.

"Yes. He specifically said so. And he's pleased with the Summer Harbor operation in general."

"Oh. Good."

She didn't go on. She wasn't sure she liked being a topic of conversation at that level. The last time that had happened, it had been a discussion on how her work was suffering because of her child's health problems.

And then, for the first time, it occurred to her to wonder what he'd been told when he was given this assignment. And just how much he knew about her.

"Did Mr. Redstone…suspect me, too?"

"Even if he did, he would never say so. Josh never sends us in with any preconceived notions. He doesn't want us biased before we even start."

"That makes sense."

"Besides, Josh never suspects anyone inside. Redstone employees are family to him."

"What if one does go bad?"

"If it does turn out to be someone on the inside, you have to prove it to him far beyond question. He always gives his people the benefit of several doubts."

"So he's as amazing as he seemed?"

"And more." He took his foot off the accelerator. "Is this that left?"

"Yes."

"I see what you mean," he said as the road turned sharply. He slowed, but not enough to make her comfortable. "Hope we don't lose him…ah, no, there he is."

"Thank goodness for moonlight," she said as he kept going and took the turn faster than she would in full sun.

She saw his teeth flash as he grinned. "This? This is a piece of cake. Try the mountains in New Zealand with no brakes. Now that's an adventure."

"You're enjoying this," she accused.

"I'm going to enjoy catching this guy," he said.

"Me, too," she admitted.

He glanced at her. "I suppose it's too much to ask for you to just stay safely here in the car, while I do my job and wrap this up?"

"Yes," she said sharply. Then, in a milder tone, "I will keep out of your way, though."

He sighed. "Bring your cell phone. In case we need to call for backup."

"I doubt if the cops will believe me," she said wryly. "I'm sure I have quite a reputation with them, after the two times I've already called them."

She only then realized that he had never even suggested they call the police to arrest the thief. Redstone, it seemed, took care of its own problems as well.

"What will happen to him after—"

"Whoa," Rand said, cutting her off as he tapped the brakes. "He's slowing down. And…turning."

Kate leaned forward to look, then frowned. "There's nothing there. It's a big tract of land some developer owns but hasn't done anything with."

"Is there a road?"

"A track, maybe. But if I'm remembering right, it's awfully overgrown."

"Overgrown enough to hide the van?"

She hadn't thought of that, only that it would be hard to drive in there. "Yes. Yes, I think so."

Before she'd even finished speaking he'd killed the engine and coasted the SUV to the side of the road. He reached up and did something above them, and pulled out the keys. Dark and silence, she realized. No dome light and no dinging door warnings. He also didn't close the door after he exited, and she followed his lead.

"Just stay close," he whispered.

"And behind," she said, her voice just as soft but with a note of wry acceptance. Rand flashed her that grin again, and her stomach did a crazy little leap.

She did stay close as they kept to the shadows of the big trees and worked their way silently toward where the van had turned. Rand clearly was picking his route through the brush and evergreens very carefully, in an effort to avoid making any noise. She tried to step just where he stepped;

if something went wrong she didn't want it to be because of her. She hoped they didn't run into any blackberries with all their vicious thorns.

He stopped abruptly, holding a hand back to make sure she stopped as well. She opened her mouth to ask what was going on, then shut it again; if he was worried about making noise walking, then talking was definitely a bad idea.

He cocked his head, listening, although Kate had no idea to what. And then she heard it, the sound of a motor through the trees. No sooner had she recognized it than it stopped. And she heard the faintest sound of voices. Plural. Their thief wasn't alone. Or it had been thieves all along.

And then Rand was moving again, more quickly now, although she didn't notice much increase in noise. The voices however, she realized, were getting louder.

Again Rand stopped, this time crouching down. She did the same, and realized she could see the van through a break in the underbrush, parked in a small clearing. She heard the slamming of two car doors almost simultaneously and then saw the two figures, one coming around the back of the van, the other coming from the passenger side. It had been, she realized, two all along.

She watched for a moment before she realized what was bothering her.

They're just boys, she thought.

This was a possibility she hadn't foreseen. And it made her wonder if she'd been right all along to suspect Mel might be involved. These boys looked about her age, perhaps a little older but not much.

They opened the side sliding door of the shop van. Kate immediately spotted the stack of familiar boxes. The two boys began to lift them out and set them down on the ground.

"When both of them have their hands full," Rand said, so softly she had to strain to hear him.

She nodded, and continued to watch. The two boys were obviously short on patience. Where they had begun stacking carefully, they were now getting sloppy. And starting to rush. And the moment came when they both started picking up two boxes at a time.

Kate felt Rand tense the instant before he moved. Still he managed to move through the brush without making a sound. When she stepped after him into the small clearing where the van was parked, she realized the two boys hadn't even realized he was there yet.

For a second he simply stood there, watching. Then one of the boys, the one who'd come out of the passenger side of the van, spotted him.

"Shit!" He dropped the boxes he was holding.

The other boy whirled. Dropped his own boxes. Stared. The color drained from his face.

"I'm outta here!" The first boy took off running. Rand glanced at him, but didn't move to go after him. He returned his attention to the driver, who was standing there as if frozen, gaping at them. Only now, that he had turned to face them, did she realize he was wearing a pair of Redstone coveralls. And then something else registered at last.

"I know him," Kate said, startled.

"I'm not surprised," Rand said, moving forward until the boy was hemmed in against the side of the van. "And I believe he knows you, too. Don't you?"

This last was directed at the boy, who squeaked out a barely audible "Yes. Ms. Crawford."

"You're Ray's son, Doug, aren't you?" she said. The boy winced. Kate looked at Rand and explained. "Ray Belker is our best mechanic. He's been under awful stress for a long time now, over his son getting into trouble."

"So," Rand said, "I presume those are dad's coveralls? That and the Redstone van made a pretty good cover. And I'll bet you borrowed dad's keys, too, so you had access to the delivery truck, including the side door."

"You can't prove nothin'" the boy muttered, but he looked even more frightened. He glanced over his shoulder, as if looking for the partner who had deserted him.

Kate, finally getting over the shock of realizing who the thief—or one of them, at least—was, put the rest of the pieces together quickly.

"It was you in the video, pretending to be working on the van," she said. "It never was the night mechanic at all, was it?"

"Video?" The boy's voice was squeaking again.

"You didn't know that, did you?" Rand said. "We've got some lovely footage of you and your friend, from the new surveillance cameras."

The boy went from pale to ashen. Again he looked over his shoulder.

"And I'll bet, when we enhance it, we'll see you and your buddy—some buddy, by the way, to bail and leave you to take the heat—moving these boxes through the side door of the delivery truck and the side door of the van."

She saw the boy swallow hard, his Adam's apple jumping quickly. She knew what the boy didn't, that Rand was bluffing. The clever ruse of parking the shop van so close to the delivery truck had hidden their activity very effectively. But it was obvious Rand had nailed it.

"Well, Ms. Crawford," Rand said, "what do you want to do with him?"

Startled, Kate stared at him. "Me? You're Redstone security."

The boy swore. And then swore again, a look of grim resignation coming over his face. The reputation of Redstone security was obviously known to him.

"Yes, I'm security, but you're the one who said it was your responsibility."

"But I—"

Rand whirled, and pushed her behind him. She nearly yelped aloud, but the sound died in her throat as a man stepped out of the trees.

Three, she thought. There were three of them. Doug hadn't been looking over his shoulder for the other boy, he'd been looking for this man.

He was tall, thin, with a receding hairline and sideburns halfway down to his jaw. He was smiling, a wide, pleased smile that was somehow chilling.

But not nearly as chilling as the shiny, silver pistol he held.

Chapter 21

"Ah," Rand said, his voice deceptively calm. "Now it begins to make sense. I didn't think those kids had come up with this on their own."

"Oh, this is too delicious," the man said, the cold smile becoming an even colder grin that told Rand that there was more to this than was immediately apparent. "One of the famous, vaunted and so beloved Redstone security team, dropped right in my lap. What a gift."

The words were curious, indicating a knowledge Rand didn't know how he'd come by. But that didn't matter now. He thought quickly. He could feel his weapon, know how swiftly he could get to it. If he was alone, he'd take the guy out right now. But Kate was here, and the man had a clear line of fire at her, so he didn't dare. He was just going to have to try and keep a lid on things until he had a chance to act without risking her. Or risking the kid who now, judging by his expression, was more scared than anything else.

Something tickled the edges of his memory as the man walked slowly toward them. He studied the face. He couldn't place him, but he was certain he'd seen him before, somewhere. He didn't know the context, wasn't even sure it had been in person, but he knew the face.

The closer the man got, the more Rand realized they were dealing with a loose cannon. He'd seen that kind of look before, an intensity and glee that spoke of a not quite normal mind. And the fact that this loose cannon was clearly delighted that Rand was Redstone security told him they were in bigger trouble than he'd thought. He'd better dig that memory out of wherever in his mind it was hiding, and soon.

He glanced at Kate. As if sensing his movement, her gaze flicked to his face for a split second, and then quickly back to the armed man. But Rand had seen enough in her expression to be sure that she realized as well as he did that there was more to this than simply a thief who'd run into a complication in his plans.

The armed man covered the last few feet that separated him from Rand and Kate. He paused a moment in front of Kate, looking her up and down. He reached out and caressed her cheek with the barrel of the gun.

Rand tensed as Kate jerked away. The man laughed. It was a very unpleasant sound. It was all he could do to keep from going for his gun, and only the image of Kate caught in a lethal crossfire stopped him. And with that came the sudden, undeniable knowledge that he loved her.

"Too bad you decided to come along, pretty lady. But since you brought me this prize—" he gestured at Rand "—I might think about being nice to you."

"Don't bother," she said. Her tone was heavy with disgust and her nose wrinkled as if she had smelled something rotten. The man glowered at her.

Don't antagonize him, Kate, Rand thought, while at the same time he smiled at her in salute to her nerve.

"Now that's not a very nice attitude. But I'm sure it will improve with a little effort."

And then he grabbed Kate's arm and yanked her to him. Kate let out a yell and elbowed him, hard. At the same time she stomped on his foot. He cursed, staggered back. Rand leaped forward. The man recovered. He'd kept his hold on Kate, and now jammed the barrel of the gun to her head, freezing Rand in his tracks.

"Now, now, getting one of Redstone's people killed would be against your precious rules."

And just how did he know that? Rand wondered. The welfare of his people had been Josh's first priority since he'd formed the security team, in fact, since he'd started Redstone and it had begun to grow. All else, he'd said time and again, including money, property or facilities, came second to the people who made Redstone what it was.

He had to poke at this guy, Rand thought. To prod, figure out who he was, what his buttons were. And how to use them against him.

"Let her go," he said. "Deal with me. Unless you're afraid to."

The man tensed and glared at him, but didn't rise to the bait. So he had at least some semblance of self-control, Rand thought.

"Oh, no," he said, digging into Kate's skin with the pistol. "She's my insurance. Redstone's private regiment won't let one of Redstone's own get killed. You run more to ruining lives."

That tickle in the back of Rand's mind grew stronger as the man spoke, along with the idea that this was somehow very personal.

The man looked over his shoulder at the frightened boy and snapped, "Get in and start the van."

The boy jumped, startled. His gaze jumped from the newcomer to Rand, and then back.

"Move!"

The boy scrambled to do as he was told.

"Now, let me just make sure neither one of you is carrying any nasty surprises."

Rand winced inwardly. He'd been hoping the guy was too lax or stupid to search them. No such luck.

He ran his hands over Kate with the same sort of salacious enjoyment that gleamed in his eyes. He gave a low growl as he squeezed her breasts. Rand wanted to kill the man where he stood for even daring to touch her, and wanted to do it in a way that would cause him the maximum amount of pain. And that was a reaction he'd never had before in his life.

Kate stood it, stoically, but Rand could see the revulsion in her face. Her reaction only seemed to provoke the man to do more.

"I'll just take this," the man said, pulling her cell phone out of her pocket and tossing it into the cab of the van. "I wouldn't want any more uninvited guests showing up to spoil the party."

The man's search of Rand for weapons was far quicker, since he had to hang on to Kate at the same time, but it was thorough enough. And for her safety, he let himself be disarmed like some green rookie. The man laughed as he yanked the .38 free and jammed it in his own belt. All Rand could think was that it sounded like a cackle. An evil, bone-chilling cackle. Keeping his tight grip on Kate, and the gun pressed against her temple, the man turned to Rand.

"Get in," he said, gesturing with his head at the open side door on the van.

"I don't think so," Rand said.

"I'll kill her," the man promised.

"Do that, and you've lost your insurance. And you'll be dead before your next breath."

"You won't let that happen. You guys are all alike, you buy into that nobility crap. Now get in."

Rand looked at Kate. He could see fear in her eyes, and the continued loathing of the man's hands on her, but there was anger there as well. He gave her an almost imperceptible shake of his head; for now, they would have to go along. He just couldn't risk making a move now. Even if he took the guy out, it would only take one centimeter of contraction on that trigger and she'd be dead.

Rand climbed into the back of the van. The man pushed Kate in behind him. Rand caught her before she fell. Then the man got in himself, keeping the weapon leveled at them while he went forward and sat in the passenger seat, swiveled around so he faced them.

"Get this thing out of here," he ordered the boy behind the wheel.

"What about your loot?" Kate asked, obvious contempt turning her voice to ice.

"It's not going anywhere," the man said. "In this case, pleasure before business."

The inference that dealing with them—or him—was more important to the man than his stolen property did nothing to ease Rand's mind. He looked around the inside of the van, looking for anything that might be of use. He saw a couple of things—some wire and a flashlight—but neither would help them right now.

"Go up the hill," the man ordered when they reached the road. "And just keep going."

Rand saw Kate go very still. Instantly, her earlier words

popped into his mind. ...*it drops off to the sound about a hundred and fifty feet.*

"What...what are you going to do?" Doug asked.

Rand saw the flicker of irritation in the man's face. He started to speak, then paused, apparently thinking better of what he'd been about to say. He looked at the boy assessingly for a moment. Then, finally he answered,

"We're going to dump these two out in the middle of nowhere, so we'll have plenty of time to pick up the boxes and get away."

"Oh." The boy sounded relieved.

Rand knew the man was lying. He could tell by the almost manic gleam in his eyes that his true intentions were quite different. He probably just wanted to insure the boy's continued cooperation until he'd safely made his own escape. Then the kid would be on his own.

If he was still alive, of course.

"What problem is it you have with Redstone security?" Rand asked, making his tone purposely conciliatory. "Maybe we can work something out."

The man's laugh was loud, harsh and vicious. "It's a little late for that. No, it's a lot late."

Okay, so negotiating was out, Rand thought.

"Where will you run to, Doug?" Kate asked the boy. Her voice was completely different than when she had spoken with such disgust to the man with the gun. It was gentler, held an undertone of concern.

"What?" The boy sounded startled.

"You're only sixteen. Where will you go?"

"I dunno." He glanced at the man with the gun, as if he expected him to have the answer. When none came, he muttered, "Someplace. Better'n here."

"What will you tell your father? Or will you just let him

think you ran away, and leave him to wonder for the rest of his life?"

"He won't. He doesn't give a damn about me."

"If that were true, he wouldn't care what you did. He wouldn't worry himself half-sick over you the way he does."

The boy looked troubled.

"Shut up," the man warned. Kate, as Rand had known she would, ignored him.

"And you know that's not true. He does care what you do, because he loves you."

"I told you to shut up!" The man lifted the handgun as if to strike her with it, even though she was out of his reach. Rand got his feet under him, ready to spring, and the man swung the gun around to point at him.

Something in the angle, or the expression, finally made the pieces tumble for Rand. *You run more to ruining lives,* he'd said. Draven. Redstone Vail.

And then he had it.

"Talbert," he said.

The man's eyes narrowed. "So. You do know me."

"Sure," he said. Right now he'd do whatever it took to keep the man's attention on him and away from Kate. "William Talbert. Draven nailed you for ripping off the resort guests at the Redstone Vail Resort."

"That damned bastard," the man said, his lip curling upward like an angry jackal. "Why couldn't it have been him they sent out here?"

So that was it, Rand thought. He had a major grudge against Draven. And since he couldn't get to Draven, anybody from Redstone security would do.

"He thinks he's so damned good," Talbert said.

He is, Rand answered silently. *He's the best there is.*

"But you're the smart one," Rand said aloud, making an

effort to sound impressed. "Nice little scheme you had going, collecting home addresses and key impressions for your accomplices. The victims didn't know a thing until they got home to find their house ransacked. And by then the trail was cold."

"It worked for years," the man said.

So Draven had been right. He had suspected Talbert had been at it a while. He'd gotten things rolling too quickly to be starting from scratch. He'd gotten himself hired at Redstone using a name and work record he'd stolen from a man he'd worked with at another hotel, and although they couldn't prove it by then, Draven suspected he'd been behind similar thefts from guests there.

"So, how did you get out of jail?" Rand asked. "The usual breakdown in the justice system, letting slime seep through the cracks?"

Talbert swore. Rand was just quick enough to dodge the full force of the man's swing at him, but the hit was solid enough to darken the edges of his vision. The front sight on the gun caught his cheek, tore, and he felt the hot trail of blood start. He ended up on the floor of the van, his ears ringing from the blow.

"No!" Kate cried out. She scrambled over and dropped to her knees beside him.

"Don't," he whispered. Her brow furrowed and she leaned closer. "He can't know."

He saw her frown, then figure it out; if this man knew they were more to each other than simply Redstone colleagues, he would have yet another weapon to use on both of them.

"Are you all right, Mr. Singleton? You're bleeding."

Her tone held the formality of a mere acquaintance. That quickly, she saved it, he marveled. He wanted to grin at her, but settled for a surreptitious wink, to let her know he was fine.

"I'm…a little dizzy."

"Oh, dear." She looked at Talbert. "You'd better get him to a doctor, fast, or you'll be in even more trouble than just for stealing!"

"Sure, I'll just do that."

The sadistic amusement in Talbert's voice told Rand all he needed to know. The man indeed planned to take his revenge on the Redstone man he had, in Draven's place.

The van began to slow, and Doug spoke hesitantly. "We're at the top, what do you want me to do?"

"Park it," Talbert ordered. "Okay, everybody, let's get out and take a look at the scenic wonders."

Kate looked at Rand. He nodded; they'd have a better chance outside than stuck in the van. He shook his head slightly; his vision had cleared, but his ears were still ringing. He could feel the blood streaming down the side of his face, soaking the neck of his sweater. He did nothing to wipe at it; the more blood Talbert saw, the more he'd believe Rand wasn't a threat anymore.

Once they were all out, Talbert glanced toward the end of the road, where a few trees clung stubbornly to the edge of the world. He smiled, that very unpleasant smile. Then he looked at Rand, and the unholy anticipation was clear in his glittering eyes.

A hundred and fifty feet, Rand thought.

"You know, I think this might just be better than having Draven himself here. Just think how he'll feel when he learns about you, and that it was me who did it." That cackle came again, and it was sounding more and more unhinged. "He'll feel like it was his own fault. He's got that Boy Scout mentality, just like the rest of you."

And he'll hunt you down and kill you, Rand thought. But if Talbert hadn't thought that far yet, he certainly wasn't going to plant the idea.

"Get them out of here first," he said instead.

"Now, why would I do that?"

"Your beef's with me. There's no reason to make them watch."

"Watch what?" Doug asked.

But Kate didn't ask. She was looking at Rand, an expression of pure horror on her face. "No," she said, her voice small. She looked a little wildly at Talbert. "That's crazy! You'll never get away with it."

"As long as they don't see you do it, if you get caught there's only hearsay," Rand said. He had no intention of letting the man simply toss him over the cliff, but he wanted Kate safe first.

"Do what?" Doug asked again.

Kate snapped at the boy. "Did you think this was all a game?"

"What do you mean? What's he gonna do?"

Talbert chuckled. "He is a fool, isn't he?"

The boy's glance flicked to Talbert, then to Rand. And then, finally, toward the end of the road where the world dropped off to the icy water. His eyes widened, and he began to back up.

"Yes, that's right," Talbert said conversationally. "I'm going to kill him. And I'm going to enjoy it."

Chapter 22

"Hey! No way, man." Doug kept backing away, his hands in the air. "You never said nothing about killing anybody. I don't want any part of this."

"Be quiet, Doug, or you'll end up next on his list," Rand told the boy.

Kate's heart was hammering in her chest. Her mind was racing at an even faster pace. Her first instinct was to protect, even this foolish boy who was neck-deep in this mess. But more important than that was the simple fact that she wasn't about to stand by and let Rand be killed. Nor was she going to save herself at the cost of his life, no matter what he said. Or did.

And the realization of just how far she'd go to accomplish that stunned her. And made her face for the first time the reason why.

The acknowledgement of her own feelings welling up

inside her, she looked at Rand. Felt her stomach clench at the sight of his bloody face. And then they locked gazes, and she immediately knew she had to postpone dealing with this; he was planning something. She could see it in his face, in his eyes, in the way he was standing. He'd just been trying to get her and the boy to safety first. And, she had to admit, give himself two less people to worry about. And his ready posture reminded her that this man was one of Redstone's crack security team, and more than likely quite able to handle a lone, armed suspect.

But a little help wouldn't hurt.

"Now, all I have to do before you take your little swim," Talbert said with unsettling glee in his voice, "is decide exactly what body part I'm going to lop off of you to send a message to your boss. I'd say your head, but that would be so messy to package."

"You're crazy, man!" Doug yelled. "I'm outta here."

Talbert looked to his right, toward the boy. "You move and I'll drop you right here."

"Instead of later?" Rand asked.

The boy must have seen the answer in Talbert's face, because he went pale all over again and started stumbling backward. Talbert shifted the gun, aiming it at the boy. Kate knew she'd never have a better chance.

"No, don't shoot!" she shouted as dramatically as she could, and ran toward the boy. Talbert instinctively turned toward her. She grabbed Doug and pulled him to the ground. Talbert took a step toward them. And for that moment, the gun was no longer trained on Rand.

As Kate had hoped, it was all Rand needed.

He launched himself at Talbert. The two men went down in a heap. They rolled, each one seeking to pin the other. As she untangled herself from Doug and tried to get to her feet, Kate could see that Talbert had managed to hang on to the gun. Fear rippled through her. Rand might be stronger and better, but that wouldn't help against a bullet.

They rolled into the shadows of the trees, and Kate couldn't tell who was on top. The fallen leaves beneath them rustled and crunched. Twigs snapped. She heard the sound of blows, and of rough, masculine grunts. Exertion or pain, she couldn't tell. She'd never seen anything like this, a real hand to hand battle with full intent. *A fight to the death.* The old phrase rang in her mind, and she knew that this was what she was seeing.

Don't just stand here, do something!

She wasn't fool enough to think she could do anything to help with her bare hands. She looked around, seeking some kind of weapon. A downed branch, a rock, anything. The only branch big enough broke when she picked it up, rotted away after months on the ground.

"Wait," Doug said, and turned around to climb in the van. Just seconds later he was back, a tire iron in his hand. Kate grabbed it and ran.

They were still on the ground. Talbert was on the bottom, the gun still gripped in his right hand. Rand's fingers were locked around the man's right wrist. It was clear that Talbert was straining to get the weapon turned from where it was pointed back toward the van, to where he could shoot Rand. Only Rand's fierce grip was stopping him.

Talbert jerked his arm. A tiny scream broke from Kate as the gun went off wildly, the sharp report echoing in the quiet night. In that same instant Talbert somehow got purchase and rolled, pinning Rand. They were perilously close to that fatal drop-off.

Kate crept closer, trying to see clearly in the shadows. If she did this wrong, both of them could end up going over the edge. Rand seemed to be holding his own, at least Talbert wasn't succeeding in turning the gun.

She thought she saw Rand glance her way. Then she knew he had when, with an effort that made him grunt, he managed to push Talbert and roll until they were a couple of feet away from the drop.

Talbert was on his side now, his back to her. With that she took her chance.

She tightened her grip on the metal bar. Swung. Connected. Talbert screamed. The gun fell. Kate crouched, grabbed the pistol by the barrel, and scrambled back out of reach. They rolled once more, and this time Rand came up on top. Talbert tried to throw him off. In a move so quick it seemed like a blur to her, he clipped Talbert across the jaw with his fist. The man gave up, sagging back and whimpering, cradling his right arm.

Rand got one knee on the ground, keeping the other pressed into Talbert's belly. Never taking his eyes off the man, he reached out toward Kate. Gingerly, she placed the gun in his outstretched hand.

He handled it with the ease and assurance of long familiarity and practice. He pulled back the metal part on top, the slide, she thought, glanced down, then let it slide back.

Talbert was still moaning. Rand slid at sideways glance at her. "Where the heck did you hit him?"

"I was aiming for his funny bone."

Rand's mouth slowly curved into a grin, and then he laughed. "I'd say your aim was pretty good."

His praise warmed her, but now that things were under control she could worry. "Are you all right? You bled so much.…"

"I'm fine. And I'm looking forward to a nice scar to counter those baby-face jokes."

She laughed then, and felt her tension ease.

"Get me that wire out of the van, will you?"

She vaguely remembered seeing the small spool of shiny silver wire, and ran back to the van to grab it. She ran back to Rand and handed it over. He unreeled a length of the wire and rolled Talbert over to tie his hands behind him. The man let out a wail as Rand pulled on his right arm.

"Shut up, whiny," Rand said. "It's not broken."

When he finished, he rolled Talbert back over. He flicked a glance at Kate, then looked back at their thief.

"By the way," he said, "that shipment you stole? It's empty."

Talbert scowled. "What are you talking about?"

"The only thing in those boxes," Kate said, "are pens."

"In other words," Rand said with evident pleasure, "you were set up. And you bit like a flounder."

And now he was gaping like one, unable to quite believe he'd been trapped so neatly. For the first time, Kate felt her pulse begin to slow. She took in a deep breath.

"I'm so relieved," she said.

"Me, too," Rand said.

"I thought...I was afraid my mentee was involved. She'd been acting so strange, I actually started watching her. Sitting outside her house, even."

Rand looked at her then. "So that's what you were doing."

She blinked. "What? How did—" It hit her then. "You were watching me? While I was watching her?"

His expression became wary. The absurdity of it hit her, and she laughed. "No wonder you thought I was up to no good."

Rand relaxed. "Speaking of kids, where's Doug? He take off?"

She had barely thought about him, Kate realized. "No, he was here," she said, looking around, "he got me the tire iron, but I—" She broke off. "Oh, no," she whispered.

She ran to the crumpled figure lying against the back wheel of the van. She saw the blood on his shirt before she got to him, and dreaded what she would find. But as she knelt beside the boy, she saw that he was still breathing.

She yanked open the front door to the van, and searched the cab anxiously. She found her phone on the floor where Talbert had tossed it. Quickly she dialed 911.

In a moment, Rand was there. While she'd been explaining where they were, he had dragged the unresisting Talbert over and tossed him in the back of the van. Then he came back to crouch beside Doug.

"I don't know what happened to him," she said, kneeling down once more.

Rand leaned over the boy, put a hand to his neck. "Pulse is steady. A little fast, but then he's lost some blood."

He tugged up the boy's T-shirt, peeling the blood-soaked fabric away from his chest.

"Uh-oh." Rand reached around and felt along Doug's back. The boy moaned slightly.

"What?" Kate asked anxiously. The boy had been partly responsible for all this, but he'd also helped them at the end, and she didn't want to see another young, precious life cut short.

"Looks like he caught that round that went off."

Kate's breath caught. "You mean he was shot?"

Rand frowned. "No exit. At that distance, it should have gone straight through."

Kate winced at the image that gave her. She didn't want to think about the fact that Rand knew this kind of thing, and probably a lot more things that never occurred in her safe little world.

He inspected the wound closely. Kate bit her lip; it was all she could do to look at all. Then he straightened up. He quickly pulled off his jacket, then his sweater and shirt. He folded the cotton shirt up into a pad and placed it over the boy's wound.

"Hold this, keep pressure on it," he said to her.

She shifted so she could do as he asked. When she had a good hold, he pulled his sweater and jacket back against the chilly air. Then he looked around, back toward where he and Talbert had been. He reached into the van and turned on the headlights, lighting the area. Then he walked that way. Kate kept quiet; this was his bailiwick, certainly not hers. In the distance she heard a siren, and hoped the paramedics got here soon.

Rand stopped at the spot where they'd been when the gun had gone off. He turned, looked back toward them. Then he scanned the area from side to side, obviously searching for something. She wondered what it was.

His gaze seemed to snag on something, and he strode forward. He knelt beside a basketball sized rock. He studied the rock for a moment in the glare of the headlights, reached out and touched a spot on it, then stood up and came back.

"I think it ricocheted. Hit that rock first."

"Is that good, or bad?"

"Probably good. Spent a lot of velocity hitting the rock. It's messier, because the bullet's misshapen when it hits, but it's probably going to save him."

As she continued to keep the pressure on Doug's wound, Kate let out a long breath. It was over. It was finally over. And at last she let in the thought that had been flitting around the edges of her consciousness, that she was glad, not that Doug had been hurt, but that Rand had not. Selfish, she thought, but true.

By the time the paramedics had arrived, she realized just how much trouble she was in. Her effort to keep her heart safely locked away had failed miserably.

"Ms. Crawford!"

Doug's expression was one of shock. He looked frail, lying in a hospital bed with an IV in his arm and various monitors hooked up to his body. He also looked scared, and she couldn't help feeling sorry for him.

"I didn't think you'd ever want to see me again," the boy said, his tone beyond humble.

"You made the right choice, Doug," she said. "It took you a while, but you did."

The boy's eyes widened as Rand walked in behind her. "Oh. I get it now," he said.

"You get what?" Rand asked.

"You're the Redstone security guy. Guess I'm going to jail, huh?"

Rand didn't answer him directly. "You want to tell us how you got into this mess?"

Doug sighed. "Man, I just wanted to get out of this place. I hate it here. It's so lame."

"So, you're saying you did it because you were bored?" Kate asked.

He grimaced. "That makes it sound stupid. It was more than that. I hate it here. My dad…we haven't been getting along. Ever since mom died, he's been mad at everything. Especially me."

"Do you know he's been here ever since they brought you in?"

A look of wonder crossed the boy's face. "Yeah. He said

he couldn't have stood to lose me, too. I didn't know he felt like that."

"That's probably why he got so strict with you. He loves you, Doug."

"He said that, too," the boy said, looking a little embarrassed.

Kate brought him back to the subject. "So Talbert made you an offer you couldn't refuse?"

"He made it sound really cool." The boy's expression said he knew how foolish he'd been.

Rand took over then. "What did he tell you?"

"That Redstone owed him, and he was going to collect. That we could sell those things for a lot of money. And he picked me to help him. And stupid me, I picked Tim to help."

"What did you get out of it?"

"He was gonna pay me when he sold the stuff."

"Did he?"

The boy lowered his gaze. "No."

"Do you know why he picked you?" Kate asked softly.

"He told me it was because I was smart," Doug said. Then, finally, he looked up at them. "But that wasn't why, was it? It was because of my dad. Because he worked at Redstone. And I could get the van, and the uniform, and the keys. That's all he wanted."

"Afraid so," Rand said. "But you were smart enough to figure that out."

"Big whoop," the boy said bitterly. "Oh, yeah, and I told him about the night guy, how he was always goin' in the back room and sleeping on his shift. Dad was always complaining about it. That's when he decided how we were going to do it."

"And he always waited up there on the hill for you to drop off the shipment?"

Doug nodded.

"He let you take all the chances, do all the work for him," Kate said. "What a great guy."

"Yeah." The boy looked away, toward the pole that held the bag of clear solution that was dripping into his arm. Then he looked back at Rand. "So…are you here to, like, arrest me or what?"

"Or what," Rand said.

"Huh?"

"You're not going to get off easy."

"I know." His voice was very small.

"I had a long talk with Josh Redstone on the way here."

The boy swallowed hard. "That's the big Redstone guy, right?"

"Yes. The one who doesn't like being ripped off."

The boy shifted uncomfortably in the hospital bed. "What did he say?"

"He's throwing the book at Talbert. Your former partner is going to spend a very long time in a cell wondering if it was worth it."

Doug lowered his eyes, and Kate guessed he was certain he was going to face the same fate.

"As for you," Rand went on, "he said he figured it would take you working for him at least until you graduate high school to pay him back."

Doug's head snapped up. "Huh?"

"And then, providing you *do* graduate high school, and stay out of trouble, you get a shot at a Redstone job."

The boy stared at him. "You mean, for real?"

"The operative phrase there is stay out of trouble," Rand warned. "Josh will give anybody a second chance. But betray his trust, and you'll regret it."

"But what about what I did?"

"Don't go thinking it doesn't matter. It does. And the minute you step out of line, those charges come back. But for now, they go away."

The boy looked away, but not before Kate saw his eyes start to brim with tears. Rand tactfully gave him a moment to get himself under control.

"So is it a deal?"

The boy swallowed hard again. Then he looked at Rand. "Ye-ah." His voice cracked. He flushed, then cleared his throat and tried again. "Yeah. It's a deal."

When they left the hospital, Kate looked up at the morning sky, which at the moment was blue and cloudless, what the locals called severe clear.

"You know," she said, "I've never been prouder to be associated with Redstone."

"There's a whole lot of us who'd walk into fire for Josh Redstone, and never think twice about it."

And just like that, it was there in front of her. His job here for Redstone was done now. He would be off to his next assignment, off to the next fire that needed to be put out, somewhere in the vast Redstone world.

When the phrase "it's over" had gone through her mind up on the hill, she hadn't taken the thought to it's natural conclusion. The relationship that had been built mostly on proximity and circumstances would also come to its natural conclusion.

The interlude was over.

And she was never going to be the same.

Chapter 23

"Where would you like to go?" Rand asked.

Kate hesitated. Would it be better for this conversation to happen in a public place, where she'd be forced to at least somewhat hold herself together? Or here, in her house, where she could freely fall apart, and hate herself for it later?

She'd taken the day off work, her boss happily okaying the time off. Everyone was happier now that the thief had been caught and much of Redstone's property had been recovered from the storage unit Talbert had rented. Each pump would have to be retested and resterilized for safety; Redstone wasn't going to take any chances, despite the cost. But it was still better than having to replace them all.

Kate had used the time off to mentally prepare herself for this ending. At least she thought she had.

Out, she thought. Out to a restaurant would definitely

be better. Because if they stayed here, she had nowhere to run. And she would spend the evening steps away from her bedroom, wondering if there would be one last night in his arms. She didn't know if that was what she wanted, or if a clean, quick break would be better.

She'd known going in that the relationship would end. She had thought that knowledge would protect her from too much pain. And she'd told herself over and over not to let it become anything other than what it was, a brief, perhaps foolish but very pleasurable interlude.

But somewhere along the line her feelings had gotten way out of control, and the pain of what was coming was already almost more than she could bear. And it was only going to get worse.

So, now you've been a complete fool twice in your life. Congratulations.

By the time they had gotten to the restaurant and ordered dinner, Kate was too unsettled to eat. And Rand was acting so darned normal it was adding to her edginess. Finally, when she'd been picking at what was usually her favorite dessert, a luscious crème brûlée, for several minutes, she couldn't stand it any longer.

"So, when are you leaving?"

Rand looked up from the bill he'd been adding the tip to. "What?"

"You're done here now. Where's your next job going to take you?"

His brows furrowed slightly. "I have no idea. I've got reports to do on this, then I suppose I'll find out what's next after that."

She tried for a nonchalant tone. "Well, it was fun while it lasted."

His mouth quirked up at one corner as he signed the

check. "This case was many things, but I'm not sure fun is one of them. I should have had it resolved a lot sooner."

Kate took a deep breath. "I didn't mean the case. I meant…us."

He set down the pen and looked at her steadily now. She had the uncomfortable feeling, not for the first time, that he numbered mind reading among his many talents.

"As in it's over now, go away?"

So much for nonchalance, Kate thought as she felt color rise in her cheeks. But she wanted this over with, so kept on. "Well, you will now, won't you?"

"There's paperwork to do, so I have to go back to Redstone headquarters, yes." His tone was flat, neutral. "What's your point?"

"Nothing. I mean, I knew it was coming, that this would never work…long-term."

He leaned back in the upholstered booth. "I see. And why is that?"

Damn it, you know why, Kate thought. *Don't make me spell it out.* But he said nothing, and she realized that was exactly what she was going to have to do.

"I'm too much older than you. I'm broke, you've got money. I live here, you need to be down south. You globe trot, I like to stay at home."

"I'm blond, you're brunette," he said.

"Don't laugh at this," she said, a little stung. "These things matter."

He was silent for a moment, then started ticking things off as if they were a grocery list.

"Your age doesn't matter, eight years isn't that much anyway. Money doesn't matter, there's enough. I like it here, so that doesn't matter either. Redstone was built on airplanes, don't forget. I can fly anywhere, anytime."

"It matters to me," she said, feeling bombarded and wondering if there was anything he didn't have a quick answer for.

For a moment he was silent, just looking at her. She held his gaze with an effort. Then a glint that made her feel very wary came into his eyes.

"Don't forget kids," he said.

She blinked. "What?"

"I want kids."

"Well that proves my point," she said. "I'm too old to start having kids now."

"I won't point out that you're hardly too old, not in today's medical world. But even if it were true, there are other options."

"Rand—"

"I want it all, Kate."

"And you should have it. So go find it," she said, even as the images of him doing just that, finding what he wanted with some other woman, made her stomach knot.

"What if I want it with you?"

Kate's heart leaped. If only, oh, if only. But now that the reason they'd been thrown together no longer existed, she knew better than to think that was foundation enough for what he wanted. She thought she'd had much more than that to build on when she and Dan had married. And she knew so much better than Rand how easily a relationship, even a marriage could be destroyed.

"You know it wouldn't work. There's just too much in the way. We're too different."

Something flickered in his gaze. She wasn't sure what it was, but when he stood up a few minutes later and said they should leave, she knew it had to have been to surrender to the inevitable.

The drive to her house was mostly quiet. And, from where she sat, miserable. When he walked her to her front door, she didn't know what to do or say. For a moment they just stood there, the silence between them stretching out like a parched desert.

And then he moved, swiftly, pulling her into his arms and kissing her hotly, completely. His mouth was relentless, probing, tasting, demanding, and by now her body knew too well how to respond. Too fast she was careening out of control, ready to throw away every bit of common sense she possessed and tell him she'd changed her mind.

And then he pulled away and released her.

"You're wrong, Kate," he said softly. "But I'm not going to talk myself blue to convince you."

And then he was gone, leaving her on her porch, going from overheated to shivering in the cold air in the space of seconds.

"Well, Katherine," Dorothy Crawford said, her voice stern, "I must say, that wins the prize for being the stupidest thing you've ever done."

Kate stared at her grandmother across the kitchen table in the house she'd grown up in. She'd barely walked in the door and both her grandparents had started in. Obviously Rand had told them…something.

"Sent him packing, did you?" her grandfather said.

"I didn't," she protested. *Not exactly.*

"Then why did he light out of here first thing, headed for the airport? And say for us to ask you why?"

He was already gone? Kate's stomach knotted. She tried to calm it, telling herself she should have expected this, that he wouldn't waste any time getting away. *I'm not going to talk myself blue to convince you,* he'd said. So he, too, knew that it would never work.

"I just pointed out how impossible it would be," she explained to the people who had been the center of her life since childhood. "Us, I mean. He and I."

She went on to give them her list of reasons why, wondering just who she was trying to convince. It didn't help any that after Rand had gone she'd been devastated that he'd given up so quickly, and spent most of the night alternately crying and trying to buck herself up. She'd finally gone to sleep just before dawn, and had awakened disgusted with herself for her own contrariness.

"And," she said at last, "he wants kids."

Her grandparents glanced at each other.

"So, you're going to let an old tragedy cause a new one?" her grandmother asked.

"What do you mean?"

"You're afraid, because you lost Emily," Gram said. "And because Dan was a miserable excuse for a human being, and made a reprehensible choice when he abandoned his wife and dying child. Because of him, you're throwing away a good man who's crazy about you. Is it worth it?"

It was the longest lecture Kate had ever had in her life from her grandmother. She stared down at her hands, resting on the table with her fingers locked tightly together because she was afraid they would start shaking.

"Do you think we didn't hurt when Emily died?" Gram went on. "We loved that child to distraction. Still do. But we also want another grandchild. And we've always hoped you'd recover enough to, if not look for love, at least accept it if it came your way."

"You've never been a coward before, girl," her grandfather said gruffly. "Why now?"

She lifted her head to look at them both. She was feeling more than a little shell-shocked. They so rarely criticized her that having all this heaped on her head was beyond disconcerting.

Were they right? Was she simply afraid?

"Are you really going to let that poor imitation of a man, who took so much away from you already, take more?" her grandfather asked.

She didn't answer. Couldn't. By the time she left them she was shaken to the core. They never lectured her like that, and that they were doing it now told her how strong their feelings were.

She drove around, wondering over and over, what if they were right?

She thought about Rand's answers to her objections. Thought about her own reaction. Thought about the pain of the days after Dan had walked out. The exhaustion of the days of Emily's struggle. The agony of the days after she had died.

So what did it mean if she let the first man to make her really feel since then get away, because of reasons that suddenly seemed just as silly as he had made them sound? And as wrong as her grandparents thought they were?

She tried to think of something else. Anything else. Tried to concentrate on her relief that Mel hadn't been involved, and discovering that her suspicious activity that day in the parking lot had been because she had cut her afternoon classes that day, and that what Rand had seen her put in the trunk was a co-worker's birthday gift she'd been taking home to wrap. It didn't work.

At last she drove out to the lighthouse, to walk on the beach. It was a bit chilly, there was always a breeze here, but she stuffed her hands in her pockets and kept going.

As she passed the white building with the red roof, it occurred to her that this was the perfect place for her right now. Where else should someone as confused as she was be but at a lighthouse called Point-No-Point? At the moment she could empathize with the 1841 sailor who had named it after misjudging how far the point of land extended into the sound.

"I think I missed the point, too," she muttered under her breath.

She had reached the end of the point. To the north Mt. Baker was wreathed in a cap cloud. To the south Mt. Rainier loomed over its domain, looking too incredible to be real, like a painted backdrop image against the sky.

She sat down on a driftwood log, staring at the mountain the Indians had called Tahoma. She thought about her grandparents, and the love they'd shared for so long. She thought about her parents, and the mistakes they'd made. She thought about her own mistakes, Dan being the biggest.

And finally, at last, she thought about her little girl. The precious child she'd had for so short a time. The child whose last words had been "I love you, Mommy." She thought of holding, loving another child. And for the first time it didn't feel like a betrayal. Emily could never be replaced. There was a place in her heart that would always belong to her baby girl, as it could to no other. But did that mean there was no room for anyone else?

She sat there, pondering, until the sun dropped below the Olympics and the air quickly turned cold. It wasn't long before she was feeling as chilled on the outside as she was on the inside.

That's three, she thought. *Three times you've been a complete fool.*

But maybe it wasn't too late to undo this one.

She got to her feet and ran back to her car. She slipped on a mossy rock, and had to scramble to stay on her feet. She dug her keys out of her pocket and had them ready. She barely remembered to turn on the heater before she pulled out. She hit the speed bumps a little too fast for comfort, but she didn't care.

By the time she got home, she had a plan.

Kate was folding a cotton sweater when her doorbell rang. She dropped it on the bed beside the jeans she'd already folded. She headed for the door, hoping whatever it was wasn't going to take too long; she didn't have much time.

She pulled the door open.

"Rand."

It came out as a whisper. He was wearing a suit. A gray one, with a blue tie that nearly matched his eyes. She'd never seen him that dressed up. She'd always thought him beautiful, but now, for the first time, she saw him as others must see him, and it made her wonder if she was crazy, that maybe he hadn't meant what he'd said at all.

"Glad you didn't forget me already," he said.

She sighed. "I guess I had that coming."

"No." He echoed her sigh. "No, you didn't. And that's not how I meant to start."

"I didn't expect you to come back," she said.

"I didn't leave for good, you know," he said. "I just needed to figure out what to do."

"Rand, I—"

He held up a hand. "Let me say one thing first." She nodded. "I can't just walk away. I'll do whatever it takes to make it work, Kate. Whatever it takes."

She'd never heard such a fervent promise. The passion and certainty behind it took her breath away and she couldn't speak. She'd thought she'd lost it all, yet here he was, handing it all back to her.

She knew now she didn't believe what had happened between them could be faked. In fact she knew it hadn't been, for the simple reason that he'd been so furious that she might have been in danger. It had taken her a while to realize it was her taking the risk that had set him off, and that was all the evidence she needed to prove that she was right. He did care, genuinely. And she also knew just how much she cared. Knew she'd slipped past simple caring and into love some time ago.

When she didn't speak, Rand sucked in a breath. Then he turned, looked over his shoulder, and made a summoning gesture. Only then did she notice that not only was there a car in her driveway—one she'd never seen before, and so assumed it was a new rental—but there were two people in it. Apparently in response to Rand's wave, they were getting out and starting to walk up the drive.

She glanced at Rand, but there was no hint of explanation in his expression. She looked back at the approaching couple. It struck her then, looking at the woman. Kate's eyes widened. She looked from the woman to Rand, and then back again. And then back to Rand again.

"'We *kind* of look alike'?" she said.

The couple reached them in time to hear her words. The woman laughed as she held out a hand. "Hello, Kate. Nice to meet you."

"Samantha Gamble, I presume," Kate said dryly.

The resemblance was truly remarkable. The woman was tall, slender, with hair the same rare platinum shade of blond as Rand. And even more amazing, her eyes were nearly the same bright cobalt shade of blue.

"How did you guess?" she asked, with a grin so engaging that Kate couldn't help but smile back. Then she held a hand out to the man beside her. "This is my husband, Ian."

Kate took the man's outstretched hand and shook it. "It's a real pleasure to meet you. And an honor."

The man looked embarrassed. Ian Gamble was nobody's image of what an inventor would look like. She knew from what Rand had told her he had to be brilliant, and she couldn't deny the intelligence gleaming in the green eyes behind the wire-rimmed glasses. But the thick mop of sandy hair softened the image, and with his sweet, rather shy smile, she could see why a woman as gorgeous as Samantha would fall for him.

"We're Rand's reinforcements," Samantha said.

"Reinforcements?" she asked, shifting her gaze back to Rand.

He nodded. "I defy you to find any couple more mismatched than these two."

"It's true," Ian said. "We're the original odd couple."

"We have very little in common," Samantha agreed. "But what we do have is the one thing that's most important. We are," she said with unmistakable conviction, "crazy about each other."

"Completely," Ian said. He looked at his wife and added softly, "Even though sometimes I still can't believe she's really with me."

There was such love in his tone that Kate felt a fierce longing she'd never known before. And Samantha was looking back at him with the same kind of love glowing in her face. Then she looked at Kate and spoke.

"And Ian had to get over a lot of stuff. We met the same

way you and Rand did. I was undercover, and had to lie to him about who I was and why I was there."

Kate's gaze snapped to Ian. He nodded. "It was hard to get past. I was pretty angry."

"I wasn't angry," Kate said. "I just felt like a fool."

Ian gave her a rueful smile. "I can relate to that, too." He looked at Samantha again. "But that's history. Now I'm the happiest and luckiest man in the world."

"Which is good, since you're married to the happiest and luckiest woman in the world," Samantha said.

"So, you get my point?" Rand asked.

Kate turned to him then. "Oh, yes, I do. But I have something very difficult to tell you."

Rand drew back. His expression became carefully neutral. Ian and Samantha glanced at each other, concern showing on both their faces.

"You've wasted a lot of your time," Kate said. "All of you."

Rand let out a long breath. "Kate—"

She held up a hand, palm out, just as he had when he'd first arrived. His words stopped. She reached behind her and pulled a piece of paper out of the back pocket of her jeans. She unfolded it and handed it to him. For a moment he didn't switch his gaze from her face, but then looked down to the paper. She saw his eyes dart as he scanned the page. Then he looked up at her.

"I was coming to you," she said softly. "I already knew I'd made a very, very big mistake."

Rand looked once more at the printout of her flight reservation. And then at her.

"Well, thank goodness," Samantha said with a laugh. "I thought I was going to have to go into my hard sell about what a great guy Rand is, and I have trouble doing that with a straight face."

"Thanks, partner," Rand said dryly.

"Hey, I was ready," Samantha said. "I was going to tell her about you getting the health fair expanded and everything."

Kate's eyes widened, and she turned her head to stare at Rand. "You were behind that?"

Rand looked sheepish. "You weren't supposed to find that out."

For a moment Kate just looked at him. Then Ian tapped his arm.

"Keys," he said.

Rand looked at him, forehead creased in puzzlement.

"Car keys," Ian said patiently. "So we can leave you two alone. You obviously don't need us, and you do have some…talking to do, don't you?"

Still silent, Rand pulled a key on a ring with a plastic rental agency tag out of his pocket and dropped it in Ian's extended hand.

Unexpectedly, Sam leaned over and gave Kate an enthusiastic hug. "Let me know when you're ready to start planning."

"Planning?"

Samantha grinned. "Yep. Redstone throws a mean wedding."

"That they do," Ian said.

The couple she already liked laughed as they walked back to the rental car. Halfway there they linked arms, and paused for a brief kiss. Kate couldn't help smiling. Then she looked back at Rand.

"Wedding?" she asked.

"I love you, and I won't settle for anything less than the best Redstone wedding yet."

Kate felt her eyes begin to sting with tears. "I love you, too."

"You know what I can't wait for?" Rand asked.

Kate could think of several things she herself couldn't wait for, a lot of them involving him being naked.

"Besides what you just thought of," he said, making her blush at what must have shown in her face, "and spending the rest of my life with you."

Her voice was husky when she asked, "What?"

"To have my new grandparents-in-law."

Kate felt a wave of love for this man well up inside her. "Then I suppose I'd better say yes."

He held up her airline reservation. "Katy, my love, I think you already did."

* * * * *

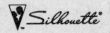

On sale now

21 of today's hottest female authors
1 fabulous short-story collection
And all for a good cause.

Featuring *New York Times* bestselling authors
Jennifer Weiner (author of *Good in Bed*),
Sophie Kinsella (author of *Confessions of a Shopaholic*),
Meg Cabot (author of *The Princess Diaries*)

Net proceeds to benefit War Child, a network of organizations dedicated to helping children affected by war.

Also featuring bestselling authors...
Carole Matthews, Sarah Mlynowski, Isabel Wolff, Lynda Curnyn, Chris Manby, Alisa Valdes-Rodriguez, Jill A. Davis, Megan McCafferty, Emily Barr, Jessica Adams, Lisa Jewell, Lauren Henderson, Stella Duffy, Jenny Colgan, Anna Maxted, Adèle Lang, Marian Keyes and Louise Bagshawe

www.RedDressInk.com   www.WarChildusa.org

Available wherever trade paperbacks are sold.

™ is a trademark of the publisher.
The War Child logo is the registered trademark of War Child.

RDIGNIMMR

If you enjoyed what you just read,
then we've got an offer you can't resist!

Take 2 bestselling
love stories FREE!

Plus get a FREE surprise gift!

Clip this page and mail it to Silhouette Reader Service™

IN U.S.A.
3010 Walden Ave.
P.O. Box 1867
Buffalo, N.Y. 14240-1867

IN CANADA
P.O. Box 609
Fort Erie, Ontario
L2A 5X3

YES! Please send me 2 free Silhouette Intimate Moments® novels and my free surprise gift. After receiving them, if I don't wish to receive anymore, I can return the shipping statement marked cancel. If I don't cancel, I will receive 6 brand-new novels every month, before they're available in stores! In the U.S.A., bill me at the bargain price of $4.24 plus 25¢ shipping and handling per book and applicable sales tax, if any*. In Canada, bill me at the bargain price of $4.99 plus 25¢ shipping and handling per book and applicable taxes**. That's the complete price and a savings of at least 10% off the cover prices—what a great deal! I understand that accepting the 2 free books and gift places me under no obligation ever to buy any books. I can always return a shipment and cancel at any time. Even if I never buy another book from Silhouette, the 2 free books and gift are mine to keep forever.

245 SDN DZ9A
345 SDN DZ9C

Name _____ (PLEASE PRINT)

Address _____ Apt.#

City _____ State/Prov. _____ Zip/Postal Code

Not valid to current Silhouette Intimate Moments® subscribers.

Want to try two free books from another series?
Call 1-800-873-8635 or visit www.morefreebooks.com.

* Terms and prices subject to change without notice. Sales tax applicable in N.Y.
** Canadian residents will be charged applicable provincial taxes and GST.
All orders subject to approval. Offer limited to one per household].
® are registered trademarks owned and used by the trademark owner and or its licensee.

INMOM04R   ©2004 Harlequin Enterprises Limited

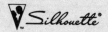

INTIMATE MOMENTS™

Coming in October to Silhouette Intimate Moments
the fifth book in the exciting continuity

No one is alone....

In Sight of the Enemy

by reader favorite

Kylie Brant

When rancher Cassandra Donovan learned she was pregnant with her lover's child, she was happy—and heartbroken. She knew that Dr. Shane Farhold's scorn for her precognitive powers would continue to keep them apart, baby or not. But when Cassie's psychic ability made her a target for kidnapping and attempted murder, Shane refused to leave her side. As they fled their deadly pursuers, their passion was reawakened—and skeptical Shane soon saw Cassie's power for the lifesaving gift that it was. But when the chase was over, would Shane be able to love Cassie completely—power and all?

Don't miss this exciting story!

Only from Silhouette Books!

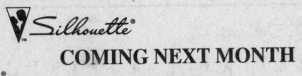

COMING NEXT MONTH

#1321 NOTHING TO LOSE—RaeAnne Thayne

The Searchers

Taylor Bradshaw was determined to save her brother from death row. Bestselling author Wyatt McKinnon intended only to write about the case, but ended up joining Taylor's fight for justice. As time ticked down their mutual attraction rose, and with everything already on the line, they had nothing to lose….

#1322 LIVE TO TELL—Valerie Parv

Code of the Outback

Blake Stirton recognized a city girl when he saw one, but leaving Jo Francis stranded in the bush wasn't an option. She had information he needed to find his family's diamond mine before a greedy neighbor foreclosed on their ranch. When his feelings for her distract him, it puts them both in danger. And the explosive secrets they uncover as they work together up the stakes—for their relationship…and his family's fortune—exponentially.

#1323 IN SIGHT OF THE ENEMY—Kylie Brant

Family Secrets: The Next Generation

Cassie Donovan's ability to forecast the future had driven a wedge into her relationship with Shane Farhold, until, finally, his skepticism had torn them apart. But when a madman saw her ability as a gift worth killing for, Shane took her and their unborn child on the run. And not even Cassie could predict when the danger would end….

#1324 HER MAN TO REMEMBER—Suzanne McMinn

Roman Bradshaw thought his wife was dead—until he found her again eighteen months later. But Leah didn't remember him—or the divorce papers she'd been carrying the night of her accident. Now Roman has a chance to seduce her all over again. But could he win her love a second time before the past caught up with them?

#1325 RACING AGAINST THE CLOCK—Lori Wilde

Scientist Hannah Zachary was on the brink of a breakthrough that dangerous men would kill to possess. After an escape from certain death sent her to the hospital, she felt an instant connection to her sexy surgeon, Dr. Tyler Fresno. But with a madman stalking her, how could she ask Tyler to risk his life—and heart—for her?

#1326 SAFE PASSAGE—Loreth Anne White

Agent Scott Armstrong was used to hunting enemies of the state, not warding off imaginary threats to beautiful, enigmatic scientists like Dr. Skye Van Rijn. Then a terrorist turned his safe mission into a deadly battle to keep her out of the wrong hands. Would Skye's secrets jeopardize not only their feelings for each other but their lives, as well?